Clara Sue Kean is currently an A-Level student living in Canterbury. *Unconditioned* is the result of her keen interest in dystopian literature and the use of psychiatry for political purposes.

UNCONDITIONED

Clara Sue Kean

Book Guild Publishing
Sussex, England

First published in Great Britain in 2007 by
The Book Guild Ltd
Pavilion View
19 New Road
Brighton, BN1 1UF

Typesetting in Baskerville by
SetSystems Ltd, Saffron Walden, Essex

Printed in Great Britain by
Athenaeum Press Ltd, Gateshead

A catalogue record for this book is
available from the British Library

ISBN 978 1 84624 107 9

For my Step-Motherland

Unconditioned: adjective.

1. Not subject to conditions or to an antecedent condition; unconditional.
2. Relating to or denoting instinctive reflexes or other behaviour not formed or influenced by conditioning or learning.
3. Not subjected to a conditioning process.

Oxford English Dictionary

Fragment One

She woke up. Where am I now? I must have been dreaming. She yawned, talking to herself secretly. Why, did I see anything? Not a chance. I must, I must . . .

'You must not see anything in your dreams. In fact, you must NOT dream.' Suddenly, a woman's voice pierced her eardrum. It was such a sweet voice, she thought. The voice, in its usual didactical tone, continued to state an unequivocal fact. 'Everything you have is everything you have *here*. Nothing else exists. Nothing else will ever exist.'

Excuse me . . . ? She wanted to ask, yet she soon found out that she had lost her own voice. So why is it? I know I am talking, why can't I hear it any more? No, this cannot be true. Obviously, I can hear it. I am having a friendly conversation with . . . She looked up gratefully. 'What have you seen?' questioned the voice, 'Who and what have you seen – in your idiotic *illusions*?' Illusion? Without any reason, this word made her shiver, as if she was sitting on an electric chair. It was not an

1

illusion, it was the . . . reality. Reality. She stood up slowly, trying to hold out her hand. Nothing was in front of her. If there had to be anything, it would be a sea of bright light. She was surrounded by this pure white illumination; gently, quietly, the sea of light penetrated her nervous system.

She saw a face, a man's face, emerging from the most concealed corner of her brain. It was a strange face. His eye colour was a foreign mixture of two unknown pigments, deep and mysterious. What's the colour of my eyes? Well, there was only one possibility. Black, the purest form of black, as if there was no boundary between the iris and the pupil. Her eyes were like two black holes, possessive and aggressive, ready to absorb every quark of energy with its indefinite gravity. The blackness in her eyes could not tolerate any other colour. It was her proof of identity. What, *her* identity? She did not have any identity. The meaning of identity is collective, NOT individual. The identity belongs to all of us. Somehow the sweet voice appeared again. Every single one of us has black eyes, and black hair. *Our* motherland is monochromic. Therefore, every single one of her glorious citizens shall be extremely proud of being monochromic. Can you remember this?

I . . . I can't remember. She murmured silently, still staring at the man's eyes. They were . . . they were so beautiful. What kind of colour is this? Is it actually a colour? She received no reply. Everything you have is everything you have here. In here, in her language, such a colour did not exist. But . . . I want to know. I want to know what kind of colour it is. I want to know how to mix this colour. I want to know . . . I want to know who you are? Where are you from? Are *we* . . . Her thought was interrupted by a slight change on the man's face. He *smiled.* This is another word that she's not supposed to know. Smile, expression, emotion. She must eliminate all these nonsense, all these 'spiritual poisons', in order to become *monochromic.* Unfortunately, he smiled at her, and she clearly knew that he did. She attempted to mimic this unexplainable change happening on his exotic face; yet this attempt eventually turned out to be a complete failure. Knowing the definition is not necessarily equal to knowing the methodology, this is how she had been taught.

Sorry, I can't do this. I can't do it any more! She cried in anxiety. Somehow she was afraid of being rejected by this strange man. Somehow she realised that he was not *that* strange. Why do you look different from me? She lowered her voice, I know you can hear me . . . please tell me that I am not alone. You are not an illusion . . . I am sure, I have been here with you before. What is the place called? Her series of illogical questions provoked no response from the man. However, his smile was still there. Like the first fragmented piece of a jigsaw puzzle, it indicated the entrance of a mental maze. She found it impossible to deduce the hidden message. I should have remembered this.

She closed her eyes, trying to drag the memory out of her skull. I am . . . with you. Once again, I am with you. She said excitedly, her black hair shining in harmony with ambient air. Even the air was saturated with bright light, creating a fine mist of white particles. You are from *the Other Place*, aren't you? Do you remember?

'You can't remember? Did you say, you can't remember, Fragment Number 29?' All of a sudden, the sea of light was ripped apart by the same voice, the sweet voice of a young woman. The man's face was deforming, disintegrating, disappearing. The colour of his eyes remained a mystery; yet she still remembered. It was such an intriguing treasure, such an insidious temptation. I want to . . . see you again. I want to . . . indulge myself in this illusion again. She tumbled onto the floor; an irritating sensation immediately froze her skin. 'Now, Fragment Number 29, tell me where you are,' the voice clutched her throat. 'Tell me where *you think* you are.'

I . . . I can't remember. I don't know. She muttered under her shortening breath with great difficulty. There are two completely different countries, that's all I can say . . . or is there only one country? The pain imposed by the ruthless voice of fact, had gained absolute control of her mind. It had the power of squeezing her empty like a tattered sponge, ready to be reformed in the factory. It could easily break her neck into pieces. To retrieve your memory, you must destroy

4

it first. The voice whispered softly, invading the last barrier in her mind. *After you have destroyed your memory, we will refill your head with our memories.*

The air particles were dancing fanatically before her eyes. *These pure white vesicles of gaseous chemicals are of no actual use, because we can remove them from the atmosphere whenever we want. As long as it is under the command of Guardian M, Our Great Leader, everything is just and feasible.* The very name of *Guardian M* was effective enough to maximise the pain, and force her to accept her memories. She had never forgotten any of these phrases; they were simply being renewed. In a confined place, for example, her brain, everything she could possibly do was to surrender helplessly.

'Now tell me. Where are *we*? There is only one country, and there will only be one country. You are a cell of this body, a member of us, The Community.' The hypnotising voice turned even softer, delivering an even stronger dose of pain impulse. *I must be ... I must be ... in ... Monochromia. Oh, no, I mean, Monochromia ...* the excruciating pain overwhelmed her consciousness, blurring the blackness in her eyes. *Oh, has she ever been conscious? Stop the pain, please, stop the pain!* She screamed in silence.

'You have committed a crime! A crime!' cried the woman's voice, 'You traitor! You have forgotten your own name, Fragment Number 29!'

She covered her face with her hands. Why, what do you mean by these words? They sound so familiar . . . ah, I think I might be able to remember now . . . it is a crime, to use the forbidden name 'Monochromia' . . . *we* have all been *trained* to call it 'Monochromia, Our Great Motherland', and there is no exception. We must utter this Noble Phrase with all due respect, and . . . and . . . my name is . . . She thought, before consciousness vanished into the air. Perhaps I will dream again. Will I ever dream again?

Suddenly the voice became calm and gentle, although she could no longer hear it. The voice condensed itself into a gloved hand, carefully stroking her hair. A woman in a white coat appeared beside her.

'It must be very cold here . . . do you not like your bed?' She sighed, holding Fragment Number 29 in her arms. She stared at her before she spoke again. 'Fragment Number 29 . . . are you my . . . ?'

Nothing is shown in her black eyes, but a gleam of pity and confusion. She slowly shook her head.

Fragment Two

Purple, dark purple. Dark purple is called violet. Violet is also the name of a flower, and a flower is . . . It is an alien word, a word that can be found in no dictionary. Nothing, nothing ever exists here.

Again and again, the voice was coming out from all directions. Which voice? Fragment Number 29 looked up nervously. What have I been doing? She sighed, sitting up reluctantly. Where am I? She asked the voice, you still haven't told me yet. Everything was pure white. She found herself in a room, a room where there was nothing but white walls. Walls and fragmented mirrors, one by one. It was like a maze with no exit. She remembered the sea of light from last time. When is this 'last time'? Perhaps it was simply a reflection created by these mirrors. A reflection of another world.

'What are you thinking of now?' The cold voice appeared again abruptly, as if it was from one of the fragments. Her heart began to race. What kind of pain will be imposed on me this time, because I've had such evil thoughts? I am not supposed to know the consequences of my thoughts? Otherwise I wouldn't be here. Here?

'Answer my question, Fragment Number 29,' the voice repeated, looking down on her impatiently. 'Are you wondering why you are here?'

No, not really. Fragment Number 29 turned back, facing another piece of broken mirror. Maybe I know why, but I don't know where I am.

'Nonsense!' shouted the voice. 'It is a non sequitur. You cannot know the reason before you know the matter itself. You must have been aware of the place to which you belong now.' Every word uttered by the voice sent a shiver down her spine. She knew it. She knew the pain was to come again, because of her illogical behaviour. She felt that her reason had left her alone. She saw the walls coming closer and closer to her, as if they would engulf her without mercy. She would be decomposed by this maze, leaving absolutely no trace for whomever. Even if her body were ever to be seen by a stranger, *the stranger*, he would not be able to identify anything.

Her elbow touched the surface of the mirror inadvertently; an electric current was immediately released from the wall, elegantly generating a black rainbow in the air. She smelled something burning.

White, pale white. White as her emaciated face, white as the sea of light that had repeatedly emerged in her dreams. Am I dreaming again, in the most alert state of my consciousness? It was no more painful for her. Electrocution seemed to be the only method of re-education that Monochromia could ever apply to her; other measures would break the law of the two colours. Black and white, and nothing else. Is transparency a colour? She closed her eyes. There was another world underneath her eyelids, a forbidden country.

A man's face. All her profane thoughts and dreams had been encapsulated in her mysterious eyes, warmly healing her bloodless wounds. Now I know why, she thought. The woman in the mirror was so happy, because she could see another image in it. Why should I envy her? That woman is not here. With great care, she tried to tidy up her hair a bit. Her black hair was obviously longer than she thought, like a polluted cascade continuously weathering her ankles. Sorry, one second! She blushed, too afraid to look at the face directly. Right, how is this? She walked closer to him, pretending to be confident. Then she saw a strange expression occurred on his face again. A smile.

'Please. Don't smile at me any more. You know, I have nothing to pay you back.' Her forged confidence collapsed internally. 'I am so sorry, Edwin.'

The last word that she pronounced, was not a coincidence. It was something from her own *memories*, her memories inherited from the unimaginable future. Flashbulb memories, she recalled the term. Edwin, it was his name, *his identity*. What's the word after 'Edwin'? It's something called . . . a 'surname', isn't it?

'Blue. Deep blue. Deep blue and green makes emerald. It is the colour of my eyes. More precisely, it's the colour of my *iris*. Iris is also a kind of flowers.' A gentle, polychromic voice landed on her withered lips. She knew that it was not from the present. Without reason, without prerequisites or hypotheses, she *knew* that these sentences had always resided in her brain. She finally remembered something that had never happened before.

The future is recurring, because she remembered his face from the deceased future. She held out her hands, forming a little cup before him. 'Can you talk to me now?'

'Where are *we*?' Edwin Iris replied, although his answer was merely another question. However, Fragment Number 29 didn't seem to have paid any attention to it; she was overcharged with excitement and satisfaction. We. Another forbidden word, if it was not followed by the phrase 'The Glorious Citizens of *Our* Great Motherland, Monochromia'. Such a phrase was not applicable here. In fact, it was hardly applicable anywhere, she thought. As long as no physical pain was induced by these thoughts, it was indeed an enjoyment to be excluded from the so-called 'Only We'. She had never admitted that she was one of that 'We'.

10

'You are from the Other Place, Edwin. We are at the intersection between these two places, and I am on my way to you. I am so frightened of leaving here,' Fragment Number 29 cried, her excitement fading away. She had never been told the name of the 'Other Place'; just like the existence of her self here, it was a *fait accompli*. She was ignorant of the mathematical location of the place, yet she had always longed to be there.

'Do you mean . . . we are not together?' Edwin frowned, but his smile was still there. 'I feel a bit confused. Would you mind if I wanted to know your name?'

'No, of course I don't mind.' She felt slightly disappointed, because Edwin *had forgotten* her name. My name is . . . my name is, Fragment Number 29. Somehow, a suffocating sensation crept over her nerve endings when she heard her own name. It sounded so lifeless. It was like a meticulously devised scientific model, precise and concise, without any emotions or external meanings. It had *no colours.*

'Fragment Number 29? It is an interesting name indeed,' said Edwin, looking even more confused. 'Is 29 your family name? Where are you from?' Edwin asked in his usual manner, casual and unafraid. She could think of no answer that would satisfy his curiosity. She did not have a family name. Nobody in Monochromia ever did. Everybody had been given a number like hers since their infancy, and the number would be reused after they died. The concept of family was a crime against the country. Forming close relationships with other fragments was almost as deadly as high treason, next to having *individualistic* dreams.

When fragments are united, they will form a new image. This is why they have to be kept apart as fragments, forever and ever. New images can only be created by Guardian M . . . she paused. Guardian M, the leader of Monochromia. *Their* leader.

'I am from Monochromia.' Fragment Number 29 looked away. She wished that she were telling a lie.

'Monochromia . . . I am sorry, I have never heard of it before.'

Have you not? Fragment Number 29 thought, staring at Edwin Iris. It was she who should never have heard of any other country; yet she happened to believe that Edwin was more trustworthy. She could not trust her own mind, not always.

After a few seconds of silence, Edwin asked carefully, 'Are you feeling unwell? You look so pale.' He stepped forward, putting his hand on her shoulder. 'Are you worried about something?'

Fragment Number 29 did not avoid being touched by him. She held his hand in her feeble grasp. Edwin blushed with embarrassment.

'Tell me.' Her voice began to quiver. 'Tell me, where are we? The place full of colours . . . are we there yet?' She finally had the courage to caress his delicate fingers, his tender palm . . . until her reason came back to command and forced her to restrain her behaviour. Nervously, she felt herself *blush*. But it was merely a feeling. She could not blush. Her skin was pale white, and it should remain pale white forever. Sorrow filled her heart to brim.

'The place full of colours?'

Even the way he talks was an exotic custom to her. However, she had no difficulty in understanding his speech. On the contrary, she found it very amiable, with an unusual sense of familiarity. Sadness could not inhibit the accumulating warmth in her hands; slowly, softly, she became much calmer. She could not verbally describe her own thoughts or feelings, as her vocabulary was strictly limited. In fact, she had already used many of the 'incorrect words'; *feeling* was one of them.

'Yes, the most beautiful place . . . your garden.'

She took a deep breath; long-forgotten place reappeared in the white air trapped between her and Edwin. It was dominated by millions of colourless flowers. It had once been her only shelter; now a godforsaken paradise, a disintegrated collection of hope and longing. Yet there was still beauty, she thought. It was destroyed by an irreversible force, when she left her precious dreams. She was reassured by such imagination.

'Oh, I am flattered,' Edwin laughed. 'I love my flowers. But how do you know about my garden?'

The word *love* sounded irritating in particular. This word could only have two subjects following it: the country and the leader. Sometimes the leader would precede the country. A trace amount of jealousy infiltrated her consciousness, causing a small turbulence.

'Probably I have dreamed of it before,' Fragment Number 29 said quietly. 'All the colours I have seen there are too important to be forgotten, because my own eyes cannot see any of them here. No colours are allowed to exist in Monochromia, except black and white.'

Edwin's eyes widened with surprise. 'Only black and white? It's so hard for me to imagine . . . but it shouldn't stop you from seeing colours yourself. In Iridescia, we . . .'

Iridescia. Her grasp tightened as a wrenching sensation penetrated her heart, spreading into the air like a black mist. Without illumination, her bleached hands seemed to have a kind of cold fluorescence. Why hasn't he noticed? Such ugly hands of mine . . . Her lips trembled with fear. He is the man from Iridescia, he must have seen the real colours of my hands . . . he must have noticed!

She had to cease her imagination. Her forearms were covered in black blisters and scars, as the result of intermittent electrocution at 'mild' levels. These wounds were there to break her dreams, as a measure of *conditioning*. They were no longer painful; they were simply a reminder. Using something traceless would be of no use. The point of conditioning is not to change, but to renew, to

14

refill. Therefore, these scars must be kept visible. They are the evidence of your own re-education. A different voice was entering her fragile brain. She knew that there was no way to resist this power.

'I am not dreaming, I am not dreaming. I heard him say the word, I am not dreaming.' Simultaneously, Fragment Number 29 had fallen into a semi-hypnotised state. Iridescia, Iridescia. The last word from Edwin, the long-awaited word, was not yet wiped out. 'Please. Let me go there again. If possible, I would like to bring another colour to Monochromia. I would like to ... render it *Iridescian*.'

The proliferating mist dissolved into an even deeper layer of darkness. Maybe it is a reflection of my own eyes, she thought, my colourless eyes.

Fragment Three

Red lights were flashing. The wailing noise of siren saturated the corridors of the State Research Centre of Mental Refilling, Monochromia. Its dedicated scientists were immediately activated, their lab coats forming a parade of white lines in the fast-moving air. Emergency! As the alarm became louder and louder, everybody in the Centre was summoned to the end of the corridor. The calmness was at its highest concentration in their tenebrous eyes; in fact, they had become much darker than usual. It was time to enforce the responsibilities endowed by Our Great Motherland, to testify *our* loyalty. There was an emergency.

However, nothing could be heard outside the building. Everything was well contained inside this concrete iceberg, serenely and peacefully. It was built in the first year of The Great Calibration, during which the idea of *mental refilling* was first proposed by a group of government scientists. It was soon proved the most effective method of operant conditioning. The actual Numbers of these scientists was a closely guarded secret; but because of their contribution, they were entitled 'The Victorious Fragments'. They had helped the government to thoroughly eliminate dreams and *dreamers*, and had reduced the length of The Great Calibration to an amazing extent. It only took ten years to complete; there were simply too many Monochromians. In fact, before The Great Calibration, no one was really a citizen of Monochromia, not even a Fragment. They did not exist until they had been calibrated *monochromic*. The Centre, proud of its expertise, had indeed played an indispensable role. Surprisingly, it had only two storeys. If there was an aerial map of the area (which is, of course, impossible), it would appear as a white hexagon, hidden in the outskirts of the Capital like an insoluble snowflake.

It had been more than twelve years since the end of The Great Calibration. It was a total success, a total success with only one exception, the inextirpable anomaly. In order to sustain the reputation of the Centre, this exception was *preserved* in the basement under lock and key, as a state secret. It was named Fragment Number 29, a potential threat to the country. The scientists in the Centre had spent nearly three years to find out the *remedy*; but there was no answer, until this week. They had eventually discovered the methodology of controlling, and, hopefully, refilling this scandalous blot. It was much simpler than they thought. Electrocution, simply electrocution administered at irregular intervals. It was difficult to adjust the voltage; whatever they would do, their purpose was not to get rid of the exception, but to reform it. It was not made to kill, although the word *electrocution* seemed to have such implications.

'Yes, to kill. To kill her mind, my compatriots.' Inside the Centre, a female scientist stood in front of an enormous white screen. Her sweet voice echoed in the room. She was not sharing her point of view; she was in charge. She was also one of the Victorious Fragments. 'Indeed, we are facing an emergency; but it doesn't mean that we have to stop doing what we have planned to do,' she continued, 'The central dogma of refilling is to expose, not to terminate. On behalf of our research, I don't think it is appropriate to end our programme at such an early stage.'

'Of course we know how to kill her mind. But you just don't let us do it,' argued a male scientist with a blank face, 'She has already met the man! If we don't refill her now, she will remember everything!'

'That's exactly why we cannot eliminate her dreams now. Fortunately, we are eventually able to wake her up,' she explained coldly, her voice still sweet and piercing, 'And I promise you, she will not remember anything. Even if she does remember something, it will never be true. Her memories have already been distorted by *our* electrocution. The real emergency is the possible result of such distortion. Will she still be able to describe her experiences with fidelity and accuracy? Will she still assist us willingly?'

Another man handed up. He had no expressions either, yet respect was clearly shown in his black eyes. He seemed to have been thinking for a long time, before he could gather up his nerves. 'Professor,' he asked, with his young, inexperienced face hiding behind his trembling hand, 'maybe I shouldn't say this . . .'

'Well, if you don't think you should say it, just close your mouth,' she glared at him with contempt. 'I know what you are going to say. Her continuous dreaming is a dangerous phenomenon, and we have to terminate it as soon as possible. Right?'

'Professor, I am speaking for our own sake . . .' the young man muttered, only to be interrupted again.

'My compatriots,' she turned back, facing the giant screen, 'she is not dreaming. She is simply obsessed with her illusions. She has been awakened from her dreams, although the reality is not yet *refilled*.' Without looking at any of the men, she began strutting around the room. 'Her illusions can only be cleaned out when she is totally conscious. Strictly speaking, she is not yet conscious. We need to utilise her unconsciousness, in order to find out what is useful for us. When necessary, we will put her back to her dreams.'

'Such a risk is unacceptable! Fragment Number 29 is a threat to Our Great Motherland, how can we rely on a criminal, a traitor, an insurgent?'

She heard someone shout behind her. She laughed secretly.

'No, she is not a threat to us. My compatriots, I have absolutely no doubt in our expertise. An emergency is merely the best chance to prove such expertise again.'

'How can you be so sure?' the man yelled in anxiety. 'How can you speak for an insurgent?'

'Don't even try to scare me, my compatriot,' she sneered again, carefully taking out a remote control from the left sleeve of her lab coat, 'I was under command.'

She pressed a *red* button, aiming at the screen. Then she lowered her head, so that she would not see what the screen was to display. Everybody in the room had silenced their throats all at once; all of them bowed down like ninety-degree set squares. Only the woman had the right to remain standing. She could feel the electrostatic charges emitted by the screen, gently attracting her short black hair. As the buzzing noise began to descend, a man's voice expelled all the uncertainty. It was a powerful voice, a voice that had the infinite ability to change and create *anything*.

'These illusions seen by Fragment Number 29, must NOT be erased.' The speech opened with a single statement. There was no response from the crowd; anyone who ever dared utter a word during the speech would be executed as an insurgent. The voice itself was a deterrent, precluding all possible dissent or objection before it ever had a chance to bud. 'However, we shall divert such illusions to a different direction, towards the *negative* coordinate.'

No emotions could be felt in the speech. Like a machine-generated programme, it functioned more logically and rationally than any human brain. It was The Highest Command. Nobody had seen the real source of the voice; yet everybody knew the fact. It was the voice of Guardian M, Our Great Leader. His omnipresent power could protect us from any danger, and prevent any danger from emerging. His command was the only pathway to eternal peace, justice and glory.

'According to the indications that have been revealed by Fragment Number 29's illusions, there is a clear possibility that the stability of Our Great Motherland might be endangered by the existence of another *non-existing* country. The information provided subconsciously by Fragment Number 29 is very, very important to the total annihilation of the enemy. Therefore, we must continue the distortion of Fragment Number 29's memories, in order to prevent her from disclosing any valid details about Our Great Motherland to the enemy.' The speech concluded with another statement. 'Remember, the Glorious Citizens of Our Great Motherland, nothing is ever a threat to us. We are the victors, forever and ever.'

The screen switched off automatically. The emergency had been successfully resolved by Guardian M, Our Great Leader. No more questions.

Fragment Four

The image on the white screen had changed. It was now displaying the status of Room Ai, in which the Centre monitored Fragment Number 29.

'Under the guidance of Guardian M, Our Great Leader,' the female scientist whispered devoutly. She held up her right hand, touching her forehead gently with three of her white gloved fingertips. Everybody else in the crowd immediately followed, doing exactly the same gesture, chanting the same sentence. 'The negative coordinate,' she said in a slightly louder voice, still facing the screen, 'Is aimed at Fragment Number 29's more distant past, her past before and during The Great Calibration.'

There was no opposition from the crowd, so she continued.

'We should send her to our Intensive Care Unit, my compatriots. As we all know, Fragment Number 29's first meeting with Ed . . .'

'Please! Help me, please!'

Fragment Number 29 appeared on the screen,

screeching and writing on the tiled floor. Her pale face had become even paler, as if the she had lost the last microlitre of white pigment in her body. There was no wound on her skin; the pain was from the inside, from a forbidden place.

The professor smiled again. How annoying, she thought. This abnormal sample interrupted her, but it is her duty to distort and destroy Fragment Number 29's memories. 'What happened?' she asked in her usual sweet voice.

'He's gone, he's gone . . . help me, I cannot see anything here . . . I cannot see him . . .' Fragment Number 29 cried, stretching out her arms.

'Look at the scars! Are they caused by electrocution?'

'We would rather call it electroconvulsive therapy, or *physiotherapy*. But the professor is just so obsessed with the term electrocution.'

'Whatever it's called, it is definitely working well.'

The room was filled with specialist discussion, when the scientists saw a close-up of Fragment Number 29's forearms. Only the professor herself remained calm. She turned to her colleagues slowly, smiling proudly. 'Physiotherapy? It sounds good. Well, my compatriots, it's time to alleviate the pain.'

Following her order, two men entered Room Ai with a stretcher. They dragged her onto the stretcher, gripping her electrically mutilated wrists. 'Who are you? Where are you taking me?'

Fragment Number 29 struggled futilely. She was staring at the men, yet her frozen eyes could not focus.

'We are helping you,' the professor said softly, glancing at one of the men. 'We are taking you to somewhere safe, warm and bright.'

The man discarded the cap of an automatic injector. Without any feeling, the needle penetrated Fragment Number 29's brachial vein. Her pupils contracted for a moment, and then relaxed like two over-stretched elastic bands. Her eyelids lowered helplessly. The man checked her breathing, nodding his head approvingly to the professor.

'Take her to our Intensive Care Unit now.'

The professor knew that Fragment Number 29 had temporarily lost her ability to respond to any kind of external stimuli; yet she decided to continue their conversation, as if it was something *personal.* 'Don't worry. You are going to somewhere safe, warm and bright.'

Fragment Number 29 tilted her head stiffly. She had no feelings. She gazed at her numb fingers, insensible to any stimulus. Her body was not restrained by any means, yet she could not move. What's happened to me? She exclaimed anxiously; no sound was uttered. She realised something different in the room. They have taken me to somewhere else, she thought. It was a much smaller room; a single bed made of stainless steel was fixed to the wall, with a liquid crystal screen connected right beside her pillow. Above her bed, the ceiling was shining ominously. The air was so heavy that she could see it drip with uneasiness. Why am I here? What are they going to do?

I was with somebody. Before I was taken here, I was looking for somebody. I was looking for Edwin Iris . . . it is so warm here. Her thoughts were repeatedly interfered by a stream of intangible sensations of warmness and brightness. Maybe I am going to stay here forever. Her breathing began to accelerate; she was too afraid to think about the possible consequence of her meeting with Edwin.

'Is your new room comfortable? It should be a lot warmer now.'

The charmingly cruel voice crept in. It was not unpredictable to her; somehow she was even waiting for the voice to come. You have been asking me hundreds of questions, but you have not told me anything so far. Fragment Number 29 replied in an undertone, looking at the ceiling listlessly. Blinding light was reflected directly onto her motionless eyes. The ceiling was transparent, if transparency actually existed. She could see the cloudy sky via this unbreakable glass barrier, although she wasn't sure if it was only an artificial image of the sky. The real sky would be pure white anyway, she said to herself. Or black. Either of these two would be the real colour of the sky. It was the first time that she could feel some kind of beauty from the monotonous clouds. She was trying to draw a line between the clouds and the sky, like a little child drawing simple geometric objects with coloured crayons. She wanted to preserve the image depicted on the ceiling. They cannot change the colour of the sky.

'We have not changed the colour of the sky,' the voice disrupted the tranquillity of the air, proudly presenting a plain fact. 'The sky has always been black. Clouds are white, this is true; but the sky itself has always been pitch-black.'

Fragment Number 29 did not dispute this statement, not even at a subconscious level. I have just come back from there, from the unending abyss of darkness. I have been flying in the sky. I trust you, she said to the voice. It is black indeed.

'We are glad to hear that.'

She looked up again with fatigue. She felt lucky that she still could rotate her eyeballs to a limited degree. Pure black, the sky is pure black. Why, where has this sadness come from? Is it sadness that I am experiencing, in my monochromic heart? The fluffy clouds began to melt down, spreading all over the ceiling. She waited for them to evaporate completely, so that she could see the real sky hidden behind them. She was in pious expectation that there would be another place, even if it was filled with darkness. The ceiling was no longer transparent; it was drenched with white liquid pouring out from nowhere. She didn't see black. The white liquid tarnished everything in her field of vision. In the twinkling of an eye, a bizarre colour permeated the centre of the white sky, rapidly diffusing. How do I know that it is a colour? I have seen it ... once again, she attempted to hold out her hand. If I could touch it, perhaps I would *remember* the name ...

Something flickering sidled underneath her bed. It was not anticipated, at least not this early. Fragment Number 29 heard a long-lasting beep, discharged by the screen, approaching her bed without falter.

'My compatriots don't like the term electrocution. They advised me change it to physiotherapy, and I agreed.' When the voice started to talk again, the beep stopped. 'You are good at testing my patience, Fragment Number 29. I was in the middle of a meeting, and you interrupted me.'

It was a simple click, followed by a compulsive scream of anguish. Fragment Number 29 could easily imagine how her body had fallen off the iron bed, how the air had become tinted with a burning smell, stronger than ever, more painful than ever. She felt as if her mind had been separated from her body; she was watching herself suffer and cry, from somewhere far above. Her skin was twisting under the effect of electric current, but in reality, she still could not move an inch. If there were ever an outsider, he would never believe that she was actually suffering. She was lying in her bed *quietly*, with a dubious expression contorted by pain. It was impossible to concentrate on seeing anything. No clouds, no sky, no white liquids dripping down the glass ceiling.

What will I see this time? I will not beg them to stop the pain. When everything is finished, I will be with him . . . Fragment Number 29 panted out the last message to herself; but it did not end as she expected.

'Do you not like your new duvet? Is it too warm for you? Just pick it up when you feel cold,' the sweet voice grinned sardonically. 'You will have a long dream, and I shall not interrupt.'

Fragment Five

It has always been black. Fragment Number 29 raised her head, gazing at the black sky spontaneously. In Our Great Motherland, Monochromia, the sky has always been black.

The sky *became* black in 2040, seventeen years after the foundation of Monochromia by Guardian M. The artificial sky, isolating Monochromia from everywhere else, was one of the most vital projects during the country's early years. Everywhere else? No, nowhere else. There is nowhere else.

Fragment Number 29 could see herself dream, yet she was only a spectator. She was dreaming consciously, dreaming of another dream. She was looking for something there. She appeared to be a little girl, her black hair tied back in a bun. She was peering through a locked window, yet her vision was obscured by a black curtain behind it. A faint noise leaked from the lock hole. It was a mixture of hundreds of different voices; all of them were murmuring something in unison. Nervousness solidified her breath. She tiptoed to the next window, searching for a gap or crack. Even the noise had now disappeared; she slapped the windowsill with disappointment, blaming herself for having missed the chance. She decided to go to the other side of the building.

It was the lecture theatre of the Re-education Committee. They were having a *public lecture* there. Eleven years later, she was still able to recognise the building. This black building, isolated from the Community area in the Capital, was constructed under direct command of Guardian M in the first year of The Great Calibration. It must have taken her a long time climbing over the barbed wire; she noticed a small wound on the girl's left arm. A viscous liquid oozed from the wound, staining the girl's white sleeve with an evil colour. The girl looked at the wound and smiled. 'I am not like you.' she said to herself *proudly*, 'my blood is not black, not like you . . . not like everybody else.'

Fragment Number 29 gasped. No, don't go there, please! She shouted at her drowsy self. The little girl did not listen to her. You will regret for having seen it throughout your life . . . she cried powerlessly. If you have to go there, let me go with you! She knew that she was to witness the event again. Every footstep left behind the girl was a segment of the most horrifying nightmare; yet she could not hinder these footsteps from reaching there. She was held back by an indiscernible barrier, a barrier created by the incompetence of her own premature self.

'Insurgent! Traitor! Traitor!'

An explosion of clamour purged all her worries for the girl. She did not have to overhear the lecture inside the building any more. It was there, it was there *for her*. The girl dashed to the main gate, panting fearfully. 'Let me in!' she shrieked, clouting the steel gate fanatically. 'Let me see them! Please!'

Fragment Number 29 had always envied the children born after The Great Calibration. They would not have remembered anything about their parents. She was born nine years before it. Although the Numbers System had already come into force, she was not called a 'Fragment' then. Her name was simply Number 29. She was sent to a collective nurturing facility as soon as The Great Calibration began. In order to become a fragment, everybody must be kept away from their family. Especially Number 29. For some reason, her parents' numbers were erased from every record, and they were the first couple of numbers to be sent to this newly built Re-education Committee. Having overheard the conversation between the tutors at the collective nurturing centre, Number 29 escaped to meet her parents.

Why have I never wondered why I was so lucky? How could I ever underestimate their surveillance? Fragment Number 29 sighed penitently. They were waiting for me to go there.

A man in black uniform appeared behind Number 29. He smiled coldly, pretending to be unaware of her existence. He watched her cry with enjoyment, until he spotted the stain on her left sleeve. He seemed to be enraged by such an appalling colour, the muscles on his pallid cheeks twitching with disgust.

'How can I help you, little *polychromist*?' the man snorted, his forceful hand swooping down on her frail neck. 'You want to go in there? Fine.'

The clasp of his hand was so tight, as if he was to uproot her neck like a withered straw. Number 29 groaned in silence, her fluttering arms sprinkling even more *unknown* liquid onto the ground. He used the other hand to open the gate.

Number 29 felt an air current blowing out from the lecture theatre, covering her face with an invisible layer of cold mist. The room was illuminated by rows of white light bulbs on the ceiling, drenching the entire place with blinding brightness. The black curtains securely insulated such brightness, preventing it from escaping to anywhere else.

I wish I were killed then. Fragment Number 29 lowered her head. She could feel sweat rolling down her temples. The girl was almost thrown into the room by the man; she crouched behind the crowd, gasping for air. Her cry was completely submerged in the prevailing frenzy; thousands of fists brandished proudly, thousands of people shouting their hearts out. It didn't take much time to regain her breath, and the dizziness caused by temporary anoxia finally faded away.

33

'Down with the insurgent! Down with the rebellious! Down with polychromism!'

Everybody's anger was targeted at a couple standing on the *stage*, located at the far end of the room. Only the voice from this couple mustn't be heard, because they were the insurgents. Both of them were wearing white gowns, and their names were written on a slate with a big black cross. The slate was tied onto their wrists by a short piece of string. They had to keep the slate hanging in the air stably throughout the lecture. Once the slate touched the floor, the lecture would be deemed unsuccessful and everything would have to start again. Everybody in the crowd was expecting the slate to drop, so that they would have more time condemning and threatening the couple, or whoever was standing there. Some words were scribbled all over their gowns, illegible from a distance.

I know these words. Fragment Number 29 closed her eyes. These words are now equally applicable to me – they have been applied to me already. Traitor, insurgent, instigator. What else? Polychromists. What have they done?

'What have they done? Mother! Father!' Number 29 screamed in despair. She had no chance to approach her parents, not even to crawl along. The room was oversaturated with people. No, not only people. It was their fury that really destroyed her opportunity to do anything. Fury, the inextinguishable fury was bursting out from their fervent throats, igniting the air like a black flame. Yet those people had no control over their own emotions. Fury or passion, anxiety or sadness, they were not the masters of their own minds. Their mechanical brains followed the same pattern, their behaviour determined by a universal programme.

The man was still standing behind her. He was seeking for a chance, too. A chance to expose this little criminal to everybody. Maybe one of them would help me. Maybe one of them could take me to my parents. Number 29 looked around the room, totally ignorant of the shadows surrounding her. Everybody appeared to be the same. Everybody was wearing white overalls, with black scarf and black boots. Men and women, everybody was identical. As the indispensable audience, these people were much more important than the lecture itself. Without them, the whole room would be completely empty . . . except the stage.

Suddenly she saw a woman walking through the crowd. She was different! She was in a white overcoat, with a black clip attached to the collar of her blouse. Is she coming to me? Is she coming to help me? Number 29 could not move her eyes away from the woman. She was almost intrigued by her elegant posture, her carefully arranged hair, and the calm smile on her face . . . for a moment, she had forgotten where she was. She had forgotten the fact that her parents were standing there. Her vision was concentrated on the woman, as if she was the only person she knew.

'Professor?' the man muttered with surprise.

She is here, she has come to me. When the woman stopped, Number 29 looked up with gratitude. Their eyes met. The woman *scrutinised* her for a few seconds, before she finally spoke:

'What is your number?'

She had a beautiful voice, Number 29 thought. Whatever she said, she had a beautiful voice. The black clip magnified her voice, signalling her message to everybody in the room, including the malevolent couple. Silence suppressed the fury; thousands of black holes were staring at the woman and Number 29. The man nearly jumped with excitement. Here is the chance!

'Professor!' the man saluted, 'she is Number 29, the daughter of the deleted numbers.'

Everybody was stunned. The daughter of the deleted numbers!

'Good. She must be useful for our study.' The woman nodded her satisfaction. She squatted down, cautiously examining Number 29's left arm. The girl was too frightened to say a word. Her entire body trembled as the woman's hand gently palpated her wound.

'You must have been told . . .' the woman said expressionlessly, pointing at her skirt, 'only black and white can survive. What's this colour here?'

The crowd began to gossip again, striving to see the girl without leaving their seats. Their agitation had gone up to a brand new level.

Fragment Six

'What's this colour here?' the woman questioned again. 'Can you not see it?'

'I . . . I don't know, I don't know,' Number 29 cried in fear. Is she really the woman that I have been waiting for? 'I didn't do it on purpose. I really didn't.'

'It is neither black nor white. You know this, you must know.' The movement of her fingers halted. Her palm sheltered the wound, as if it had a healing power. 'Shall I make it more obvious for you?'

The wound reopened in a gentle flow of *something warm*. It dripped down the woman's left hand, contaminating her white overcoat. She pulled out her forefinger from the wound carefully, holding it still before Number 29's afflicted eyes.

'Can you recognise it? Look, you've got a lot of it now.'

The pain grew more and more severe, as the questioning continued. 'Sorry, I don't know, I don't know! What are you expecting me to say? I don't know!' Number 29's childish voice weakened, as if it was being drained away from her body.

'We are not expecting you to say anything,' said the woman, with a satisfied smile. 'You are not allowed to say anything. Now, tell me, what is this colour called?' She looked back, towards the audience. The liquid slowly trickled down like the sand in a malfunctioning hourglass, acting as a representative of *incorrectness.*

Everybody was speechless; they were too shocked to have any answer. This wicked girl had brought in another colour! She was here to challenge the singularity of Our Great Motherland! No wonder she was the daughter of the deleted numbers!

'Anybody?' the woman waved her hand, as if the vicious stain on her palm was a trophy. 'Shall I tell you then? It is called . . .'

'Polychromism, my compatriots. It is called polychromism.'

A man sitting in the last row broke the ice. His voice was amplified by a microphone, too. 'Well, I don't think it's necessary to keep silent any more, my degenerate couple of numbers. It must have been very difficult . . . watching your own daughter suffer like this.'

No! Don't move, mother! Fragment Number 29 whined instinctively, in another ineffectual attempt to sway the situation. Please! Don't move! You will drop your slate . . .

'Mother?' Number 29 sobbed semi-consciously when she heard the man talking to her parents. She wanted to stand up, yet it was too painful to move. 'Are you there? I know you are there, mother . . . help me . . .'

'My daughter! Yes, I am here, I am coming!'

As Number 29's voice disappeared, one of the deleted numbers collapsed at last. Her body rolled down the stage, whereas the slate was still attached to her slender wrists. The force exerted by the string lacerated her skin; something dark spattered the slate.

'No, don't go!' her husband cried out, almost short of breath. 'Please! We'd better . . . Oh, please . . . my compatriots! I am innocent! It was not my idea to write . . . I am innocent!' As he tried to grasp her arm, he tripped over. His slate fell onto the floor.

'Behold! They've dropped their slates. They are going to *reunite* with polychromism! Stop them, my compatriots!'

The man's voice had been transmitted to nobody. Under the man's command, everybody darted to the stage without losing the regularity of their footsteps. The crowd had retrieved their collective bravery; the room was deluged with tumult, where anybody could wreak his vengeance on the enemies of the country. Many of them had never met the couple in person, but it would not affect their resentment. On the contrary, the strangeness of the enemy had intensified the excitement of revenge. Only very few people were informed of the crime that they had committed; none of them had been offended by the couple. It did not matter! Accuse them! Condemn them! Attack! Revenge! Anybody who refused to take part would be judged as an accomplice, so beat them up! Demonstrate your love for Our Great Motherland, prove your innocence and loyalty! Attack! Revenge! Eliminate them!

'In the name of Guardian M, Our Great Leader! Down with . . .'

The man did not have to finish off the slogans; the crowd knew very well what they were supposed to say. These people were like a cassette recorder: all you had to do was to plug it in, turn the knob and speak to it. Only once will do; it has an amazing capability of memorizing things, whatever they are. When you need to use it next time, simply put the cassette into the slot. This is exactly what the man did. Shouting the first few words of the slogan, and here we go! The cassette is working perfectly. What's better, you can easily erase the recorded content and reuse them! How environmentally friendly!

So, what if there is a defective cassette? What if it is not black from the very beginning? What if you are unable to scrap the original recording? Well, it's not a problem. *We* will purify it.

40

'Thank you very much for your demonstration, professor.' The man shuffled out of the crowd, smiling at the woman. 'I am the lecturer. Is their response up to your expectations?'

'Oh, of course it is. Better than I thought. I am pleased with the *flexibility* of these people.' The female professor shook his hand (with the unstained side). 'Is this your first lecture?'

'It is the first one in the Committee, to be honest,' the lecturer frowned. 'Luckily we do have some bonus. Why is Number 29 here? Shouldn't she be in the collective nurturing facility?'

'We are working in collaboration with those facilities. I thought it would be useful if Number 29 could witness the re-education of her parents. According to her tutors, she is a difficult case.' The professor shrugged her womanly shoulders. 'Hopefully today's event will have some influence on her rebellious brain. At least it appears to be effective, although we still need further observation. Her collective nurturing facility is not doing a great job, I am afraid. Therefore, we have been contemplating the possibility of transferring Number 29 to our Centre.'

'What? She is only a little girl!'

'So? Our research has just begun! You know, young children are supposed to be malleable. Look at her! Where else can I find such a negative example? My compatriot, she has to become a fragment, sooner the better. Many of the children at her facility have become fragments already.

Don't show off your sympathy before *my* eyes. I know you are more excited than anyone else in this room.'

'Professor, your left hand . . .' The lecturer tried to prevent further contamination on the professor's overcoat.

'Ah, you mean this? I wish one day we could all bleed white, or black.' She looked at her left palm with great interest. 'But, my compatriot . . . do you not find it *lovely*? I have always wondered . . . haemoglobin has a tempting colour.'

'Because of the iron in it.'

'That's right,' the professor laughed approvingly, 'by the way, do *you* know why Number 29's parents are the first couple of numbers to be re-educated?'

'No . . . not really,' said the lecturer, looking slightly embarrassed. 'They are polychromists, that's all we've been told.'

'They are not ordinary polychromists. They are novelists. Do you know what that means?' Having received a negative reply, the professor continued her explanation calmly. 'They make things up. They encourage people to imagine, to dream. Polychromic dreams.'

'Wh-what?' the lecturer stammered, 'no wonder Number 29 is such a hot potato.'

'Everything I do has a reason. I am sure her collective nurturing facility would be dying to get rid of her, had it been involved in our conversation. I will further negotiate with the facility later. She will not have an easy time there anyway. The truth about her parents' re-education will be declassified soon. Can you think of the possible response from the facility? Her tutors will rip her heart apart. It is the worst thing on earth, to have the child of two polychromists *of this kind,*' said the professor, pointing at the far end of the room nonchalantly. 'It's gone really *messy* now. Don't tell me the deleted couple are already dead.'

I have chosen to dream. Fragment Number 29 thought, Nobody is dead *yet*. Somehow, she felt proud when she discovered that Number 29 was still lying on the floor. *We* have chosen to dream.

Fragment Seven

'The word *we* is not only inclusive, but also collective. The most important thing is that you must be aware of the *singularity* of this collective we.'

Number 29 was having a lesson in her collective nurturing facility, together with all the other little numbers. As the *eldest* Fragment-to-be in the facility, she had to sit in the last row of the class. This was to prevent her from asking questions. Most of her classmates had not yet learnt how to speak; their skills of language had to be taught by the facility, so that their vocabulary could be strictly controlled. Everything said by their tutors would cauterise their raw minds into a solid, monochromic brick. They had neither the intention nor the ability to wonder, to ask; their only duty was to listen.

The classroom was painted purely white. Compared to the Re-education Committee, the white appearance of the collective nurturing facility somehow indicated *innocence*. Their uniform was white, too. White blouse, white skirt, white opaque tights and white bootees. When Number 29 was handed over to the facility after the public lecture, none of her tutors volunteered to issue her a *clean* skirt until a memorandum was delivered to its central office, stating that it was necessary for the progress of The Great Calibration. The nurse on duty had to wear triple-layered rubber gloves to bandage Number 29's left arm. 'I wish I could incinerate her clothes when she's still wearing them,' the nurse grumbled for the rest of the day.

'Only guilty numbers will be sent to the Re-education Committee. We are the innocent numbers. Look at this room. It represents our unity, because it is white. Only innocent numbers have the right to stay in a white room like this. However, even white numbers have to be educated to become fragments,' the tutor continued in her mechanical voice, squinting at Number 29. 'What we need is education, not re-education. We are the *hopeful*. We have both the desire and the opportunity to learn.'

Number 29 listened with no expression. She was the contaminated one. She was something to be ashamed of, something to be got rid of sooner or later. She knew the significance of silence. Either keep silent yourself, or be kept silent forever. She looked up when the tutor had moved away her attention from her.

White, the ceiling is white. It was meant to be white, but . . . Number 29 *thought*. Her mind was never silent. Before she was transferred to the

State Research Centre of Mental Refilling, nobody could disturb her *thinking*. Everything I see here is black. The ceiling, the floor, the window frames, the curtains . . . everything I see is black, everything around me is black. The sky is black, but I do remember . . . there had been other colours in the sky.

'Our Great Motherland, Monochromia, is the only country in the entire universe. Civilisation has favoured nowhere, but Our Great Motherland. All of us should know why we are so gifted.' The tutor raised her right hand, touching her forehead with three of her faithful fingertips. 'Because of Guardian M, Our Great Leader. He has brought us everything. He has created the existence of everything, including us. How lucky we are, to be monochromic from our birth!'

All the little numbers nodded their algebraic heads, except Number 29. Monochromic? What does it mean? Black and white? So why is it, that I can see no whiteness here? Black, everything is black. She looked up to the ceiling, as if her field of vision could go beyond the white barrier above her. They don't know anything. She thought, glancing at her classmates. Before they were born, there had been many other colours . . .

'We have black hair and black eyes, and we dress in white,' the tutor said proudly. 'We must be grateful, for everything given by Guardian M, Our Great Leader. He is protecting us from contamination by any other colour. In fact, there is no other colour. They don't exist, and they will never exist anywhere.'

Yes, there is, there is. I saw it, I saw it yesterday! Number 29 clamoured in silence. I don't know what it is called, but I saw it coming out of my body. *A different colour.* It is inside me, I saw it!

'Unfortunately,' the tutor put down her arm, slowly shuffling towards the other end of the classroom, 'not every number is as well-educated as we are. Their minds are already discoloured by ingratitude and individualism. They refuse to become fragments, they refuse to be calibrated.' A gleam of resentment came into her eyes as she reached Number 29's seat. 'We are responsible for the inevitable success of The Great Calibration. It is our duty to do whatever we can to calibrate these depraved numbers. None of us will ever be convinced that there are such numbers who call themselves *I*, instead of *we*. Remember, using the pronoun I is a crime against Our Great Motherland. A crime!'

Everybody shivered when the tutor uttered the word *crime* with a factitious screech. She was evidently pleased with the effect she had inflicted on these incomplete fragments. 'Does anybody know what will happen to those criminals in the end?'

If these little numbers had been able to speak, she would have never asked such a question. Number 29 scoffed at her secretly. The bandage on my arm can overthrow everything that you have tried to fill me up with. Who is this *we*? *You look at least forty years older than me.*

'They will be deleted,' the tutor chuckled. 'We will purify them first, and then delete them in the Re-education Committee. Isn't it an effective process, Number 29? Yesterday's public lecture must have been very *amusing.*'

Everybody's attention immediately converged onto a single point. Number 29 was bewildered by her tutor's blitz tactics, gaping at her classmates speechlessly. 'I have been silent throughout the lesson!' her perplexed eyes watered in grief, 'what have I done? What am I supposed to say?'

'We adjure you to tell us, Number 29,' the tutor stressed, 'tell us why you went there.'

I cannot say anything. Anything I say will be used against me, so I cannot say anything! Number 29 winced, embracing her head with her defenceless arms. It was a place full of horror and darkness, a place where I met a strange woman . . . she was holding her hand before my eyes, and an *aromatic* liquid was dribbling down . . . I saw my mother and father there, I saw the same liquid pouring out from my mother's hand . . . I don't want to remember, I don't want to remember!

'I am not telling you! I am not telling you!!'

Number 29 screamed hysterically; her consciousness was on the verge of total collapse. Yet she did not pass out. Her bandaged arm was pinned back by her tutor's powerful grip, as if she was to dislocate her elbow permanently.

'Scandalous! We have all heard what she's just said, haven't we? She has used the word *I*! She has committed a crime!' the tutor yelled, pinching Number 29's injured wrist spitefully, with incredible accuracy. 'We know that she is *dirty*; her parents were deleted numbers! Every one of us must keep away from her, she is a guilty number! Guilty!'

'Why don't you send me to the Re-education Committee as well? If you don't want me to exist anywhere, why don't you get rid of me?'

Her junior classmates immediately glared at her with anger and disgust; numberless accusations perforated her obnoxious body, although none of the accusers could speak a single word. Number 29 felt something wet underneath her bandage. Nothing is happening. She bit her lips desperately, in the last attempt to hypnotise herself. I am not here, I am not here, I am not here. I can dream, I can get out of here in my dreams. That's why I have chosen to dream forever. To escape from 'we', to escape from all the misery, and find somewhere safe . . . there must be another country.

Fragment Number 29 opened her eyes in a spasm of pain. Everyday in the collective nurturing facility was a repetition of the same 'lesson'. My wounds had never recovered, never. I was born to be a target, I was born to be eliminated . . .

'We will not eliminate you, Fragment Number 29. It seems that you have dreamt of our first meeting. I hope my first impression is not too bad.'

The professor's sweet voice dripped rhythmically from a plastic sack hanging above Fragment Number 29's bed. She had a bizarre feeling that the sack was floating in the air, without any support. A white rubber tube connected the sack to her right arm. There was no wound, no bandage, but a black needle half-covered in white gauze and plasters. It was not a dream.

Fragment Eight

It was a magical drug. Thank you, professor.

Fragment Number 29 whispered to the screen with an appeased look. Perhaps I don't have to dream any more. Why, was it really a dream? I met my parents there, and I saw a little girl outside a black building surrounded by barbed wire. Everything seems to be so far away now.

'Do you feel any better now?' The screen buzzed; millions of black and white dots began to unite, forming one single image. A woman's face gradually emerged behind an invisible glass wall, between Fragment Number 29 and the strangely familiar woman. Fragment Number 29 gasped. She could not associate the sweet voice with any virtual image, until this moment.

Nothing had ever changed in the last eleven years. She is still so beautiful, her voice still so melodious. It is her charming voice that has monitored me constantly, Fragment Number 29 thought. She dared not move her eyes away from the screen too hastily. It was such a lively image;

she tried to match the woman in her dream with this image, the more detailed the better. The professor was gazing at her, as if she was waiting for Fragment Number 29 to decode what was hidden behind her silver-rimmed spectacles. She was still wearing her hair in a chignon, with a ringlet carefully pinned beside her right temple like a black ribbon. A ringlet? I did not see it at the public lecture. Everybody's hair must be straight, not curly or any other form! Why does she have a ringlet?

'Fragment Number 29? It is my second question already,' the professor spoke again, in an exceptionally gentle manner. 'How do you know it's called a ringlet?'

Fragment Number 29 had no answer. Anything I say will be incorrect. She wanted to shake her head, yet her body was completely stiff. All she had was her sensory memory, and the woman on the screen controlled everything else. I have to say something, otherwise . . . my feelings are not lost yet. If they do anything to me again . . . no, they won't. At lease she won't, because she had always been taking care of me.

'Because I . . .'

It was a sweet voice. Where did it come from? Fragment Number 29 searched around within her limited visual field nervously. It sounded familiar, but the word *I* does not exist . . . it must have been from nowhere. 'Professor, please trust . . .'

'This sentence has to finish with the word me,

Fragment Number 29. It is not a crime to use such words. *Not here.*' The professor smiled. 'Don't be scared. It is *your* own voice.'

My own voice? Fragment Number 29 stared at the sugary traces left in the air when the voice landed on her white duvet, as if she was shocked by something alien. My voice is never this sweet. It is yours, professor. It must be yours.

'Yes, it is yours indeed. Now we have returned your voice to you, so you don't have to speak in silence any more.'

Although the signal was interfered by one or two unstable electrons behind the screen, the voice was still clearly recognisable. It was her own voice, yet in a lower pitch. There was a sense of calmness in that voice, which had never belonged to her. Fragment Number 29 felt a little *ashamed* because her voice possessed an extreme similarity to the professor's. She took a deep breath before she could be brave enough to open her lips again.

'But why? Why do I have this voice?'

'It is our compensation,' explained the professor, looking slightly disappointed, 'because you will be paralysed like this for a very long period of time.'

What is the purpose of this? Fragment Number 29 frowned motionlessly, repressing her sinful curiosity. She was not afraid; for some reason, she felt that it was much more comfortable in her bed. Maybe *we* can have a friendly conversation here. The liquid was dripping continuously from the plastic sack; she could see the volume decrease, microlitre by microlitre. It was a transparent liquid, innocent and unrestrained, just like her new voice. This compensation is more than I deserve. If I could, I would like to smile at the professor in the way that she has always done to me. I haven't answered her questions yet. How ungrateful I am.

'Professor, I am sorry . . . I have *forgotten* your questions. Could you come closer to me? I do feel . . . much better now.' Fragment Number 29 blinked at the screen. Although with difficulty, she noticed that there was somebody else standing behind the professor. The image stepped forward, occupying the entire screen. I am sure we will have a friendly conversation here.

'Is this close enough?' The professor smiled again, as if she was facing a camera, ready to be captured in a graduation photograph.

'Yes, very close. Thank you, professor.' Fragment Number 29 hesitated for a moment before she could carry on the chat. 'I like your hair, professor. Especially the ringlet. It makes you . . . so special. I know it's called a ringlet because . . .'

Fragment Number 29 paused abruptly. I cannot remember, she thought. Why do I know it? I am not supposed to know anything at all. Something heavy was pressuring her wheezing chest, squeezing her lungs empty. Help me, professor. Only you can recall my forgotten remembrance.

'Don't worry, Fragment Number 29.' The soothing voice immediately relieved such pressure before it could cause any further damage. The professor touched the other side of the screen, as if her body temperature could be conveyed to Fragment Number 29, to repair her lost memories. 'I was born with it, and I have the *privilege* to keep it.'

'Privilege?' Fragment Number 29 quivered. This word was not meant to be uttered, if it had ever existed. It should have been deleted from the dictionary years ago, even before The Great Calibration. Why do I remember its meaning?

'You are privileged here as well, to use prohibited words like *I* and *my*. Privilege does exist in Monochromia, Our Great Motherland. You are privileged because you are here, in *our* Centre.' The professor's voice became more tranquil when she pronounced these words herself. 'You are special. You are different from everybody else in your collective nurturing facility, so we think that you are eligible to be privileged in the Centre.'

'You have always been with me, professor, haven't you? Wherever I go, you are always looking after me.' Fragment Number 29 sobbed quietly. The maternal figure on the screen was intangible, yet she could not disobey the desire to reach for it. 'Professor!' she raised her voice instinctively after a short pause, 'are you my . . . ?'

'Where have you been? Where have you been . . . *with me*?'

The professor's smile interrupted her thought. Even this smile was tinted with some kind of strange familiarity, yet Fragment Number 29 had already forgotten her previous question. Here, here. Please, let the image freeze here. Your smile is too beautiful to be true, too amiable to be preserved. Your smile had led my way incessantly, to many different places. And your sweet voice, your flawless face. How could it be, that I had once resisted your kind assistance? I would never have seen *the third colour*, had you not introduced it to me at that lecture . . . I would never have visited . . .

'Iridescia,' Fragment Number 29 mumbled, her lips trembling with sorrow, 'can you remember, professor? *We* have been to Iridescia . . . and we have met a man there, his name is . . .'

'Iridescia? Of course, I remember,' nodded the professor, as if she was talking about a remote acquaintance. 'You miss him, don't you?'

I thought I would forget about him, after all the horrible dreams that I've had. Fragment Number 29 narrowed her eyes; the plastic sack floating above her became more and more slender. A beam of white light sneaked through the glass ceiling, its warmth covered every corner of the room. The screen flickered brilliantly, puncturing the most sensitive point in her unbalanced heart. I have so many things to tell him. I didn't even say goodbye last time . . .

'So there is another country! You have been there with me, to the other country!'

Her voice was neglected as the last drop in the

sack fell into the black tube, like a blind passenger wandering in a deserted tunnel. The image of the professor began to dissolve.

'No, there is not. There is only one country, and only one single we.'

The professor's enchanting smile was enervated by her last message; instead, an insidious grin reappeared on her snow-clad face. She removed the ringlet, gently and artfully. The person standing behind her snorted.

Fragment Nine

A white cloud slowly emerged from the other side of the screen. The professor stood still, her bleak eyes tracking down the trail of the cloud alertly. It will reach her soon. The professor thought, When it has been filtered thoroughly.

'We shall divert such illusions to a different direction, towards the *negative* coordinate.' Suddenly, her field of vision was obscured by a man's hand, a hand shrouded in black leather. She turned back reluctantly, with her hands clasped behind her white coat. She scowled at the man sullenly.

'The Centre has been very successful in achieving this target. We shall be very proud.' The man continued without looking the professor in the face; his hand came even closer to her watchful body. 'However, I am afraid that I have to ask you a simple question.'

'Oh, please do,' she replied impassively. 'Is it about . . . this cloud?'

'You are always so perceptive, my compatriot,'

the man smiled, his black palm finally landed on her left shoulder. 'Are you sure you want Fragment Number 29 to meet the man again?'

The cloud had already begun its journey. It would fly over the selectively permeable membrane between the meeting room and the Intensive Care Unit, and infiltrate Fragment Number 29's hippocampus. Everything she needed to know was condensed and contained in this cloud. 'It is *not* my decision. The Centre acts under direct command of Guardian M, Our Great Leader.' The professor said in a reconciled tone; her tensioned pupils began to relax. Once the cloud had entered the screen, there would be nothing for her to worry about.

'I am the inspector!' the man shouted his discontent. 'It is not what I expected to hear. Why don't you refill her straight away? Why do you have to wait until she has gone through all these useless processes?'

'Don't argue. Remember, this is not a private conversation.' The professor laughed, glancing at the white screen. 'I was not expecting such an inspection either, my compatriot. Anyway, I do understand why you would like to come back here.' Her eyelids lowered, curtaining her bottomless eyes. 'After a certain event.'

'A *certain* event? I hope you know what you are talking about. I have never imagined that you could reach such a high position here . . . without *that* event!'

'You are absolutely right, my compatriot,' the professor replied calmly, 'now I am in charge. Sometimes, the unpredictable becomes the most fascinating thing in your life. I have never imagined that you would ever leave the Centre for . . .'

The last few words ignited the sole trace of reason remaining in the man's brain; his enraged hands shuddered. The professor nimbly slipped away from his incapacitated grip. She knew that she had rubbed some salt into his wound again. Not a bad idea, is it? She laughed at the man with a spitefully delighted look. He was a young boy in black uniform, an over-enthusiastic boy. I should never have taken him in. 'But now you are the inspector for the Centre. Doesn't it feel good?'

The man snorted heavily, as if all his energy was to be evaporated in his nose. 'It is all your fault! You called it a *secondment*. You know better than anybody else in the Centre . . . all you want is a scapegoat, if anything goes wrong!' The vapour released from his nostrils formed a sinister smirk. 'Yes, of course I do have the power to inspect your Centre . . . so answer my questions *now*! Why do you not carry out the normal procedures? Why do you send Fragment Number 29 to . . .'

'To where?' the professor questioned emotionlessly. 'Do I have to tell you again? It is not a private conversation. She is going to nowhere, my compatriot. Nowhere. And nothing will go wrong, I can assure you.'

'Are you sure? I don't believe a word. Don't forget what you had told me about your research . . . although you are a Victorious Fragment, you are never an *integer*.' He deliberately weakened his voice while emphasising on the phrase 'Victorious Fragment'. 'Don't forget who the first subject was for your experiment. Don't forget how you *became* a Victorious Fragment! At the Capital University . . .'

'I have never forgotten, and I will never forget.' The professor smiled *warmly* with her saccharine voice, as if she was to make caramel out of the vibration of air. 'All these things that you are now striving to remind me of. May I make a simple correction?' she asked in a kind of threatening equanimity, yet she did not wait for the man to respond. 'I have always been a whole number, an integer. Before I was entitled a Victorious Fragment by Guardian M, Our Great Leader, I was called Number Nil.'

She held up her right hand. The artificial ringlet was still lying there, serenely and sincerely. She gave it a nostalgic glance, and buried it in her pocket.

'What is your purpose? Professor, why are you doing all these?' The oppositional force retreated cowardly. His fury was compelled to descend; his line of sight fluctuated fearfully. 'Who are you?'

'I wouldn't trust you if you told me that you suffer from short-term memory loss,' the professor shrugged. 'I am Number Nil, a Victorious Fragment.'

There was a short pause.

'I think the cloud has arrived at its destination. Would you like to join *our* observation, my compatriot and former colleague?'

'Where am I? I am going nowhere.'

Fragment Number 29 stumbled along the soft path in the cloud. She was walking on a path of light. Here was the sea of light, her own sea of light. It is the crossroad between two antagonistic places, and she felt that it would take her somewhere.

'Now ... I have my own voice. I can hear it myself. I miss the place *we* went last time. I miss someone there.'

She knelt down, carefully holding a handful of the mist surrounding her. She could see the particles dance, like millions of intangible fireflies. What are they, she thought, fireflies? They emit light in a different colour, but all I have is white, dazzling white. I must ask *him* what it's called.

'Are you waiting for me? Have you been waiting long, Edwin? We have promised to meet up here ...'

Once again, she tried to comb her hair palely with her fingers. He is coming soon. The luminous confetti in her hands scattered when she opened up the capsule, bouncing and rolling all over the place.

'Ah, don't go . . .'

She jumped up to seize the particles, waving her white sleeves impatiently. She didn't realise that she was rumpling her hair instead of arranging it. She had not experienced the feeling of chasing after something for a long time. Her senses became lighter and lighter, as if she was to float in the air as well. Following the footsteps of these prophetic droplets of light, she had arrived at her destination.

'Fragment Number 29? I have been looking for you.'

She saw a pair of *cucumber green* eyes. His colourful voice rendered the entire cloud melodious. Are you really Edwin? Have you really come for me? An appealing sensation filled up her airway; she blinked and blinked again, as if the movement of her eyelids would deform the image of this man.

'Edwin? Are you . . . Edwin Iris?' she exclaimed. 'Is it really you?'

'Of course it's me, Miss Number,' Edwin beamed with delight, his foreign-coloured glowing excitedly. 'I am so sorry that I lost my way last time. It wouldn't have happened if I'd been given a map. Anyway, how are you feeling? You looked upset then.'

'I feel . . . much better, because I can meet you again,' Fragment Number 29 tenderly shook her head. 'But, Edwin . . . I am not Miss Number. My name is Fragment Number 29.'

'Ah ... I am so sorry, Miss 29. Your middle name is a bit too long for me.' Edwin stuttered, scratching his falsely pigmented hair. 'Please don't take offence.'

Middle name? Another word with oblivious familiarity. What is Miss 29? She gazed at him with bewildered eyes, Have I told you the wrong name? 'Edwin, I am not Miss 29. Please call me Fragment Number 29.'

'But ... ah, I forgot. You are from a different country, no wonder you can't understand what I meant . . .' Curiosity displaced his question as he suddenly recalled his last conversation with her. 'Did you say, you are from Monochromia?'

I don't know what to say. I cannot remember what I told you last time. Fragment Number 29 frowned, twiddling her fringe nervously. She waited until she had inhaled enough air to withstand the pressure induced by such nervousness. 'I don't know what I said, Edwin ... but I do remember that you are from Iridescia, when you lost your way . . .' The pace of her speech hastened after a few seconds of silence. 'Edwin, I just want to make sure ... have you ever heard of Monochromia before? You have not, have you? Have you? Iridescia is the only country, isn't it? Tell me! Please!'

'Oh, please calm down, Fragment Number 29 . . .' Edwin grasped her wrists, yet he was not shocked by her over-reaction. She was like this last time. Why does she look so scared? 'I have not heard of Monochromia before, and my nationality is truly Iridescian.' He looked at her compassionately, brightening her pale skin with a polychromic tone.

Fragment Ten

You have never heard of Monochromia before. Fragment Number 29 was astonished by such an immediate reply. He must be telling the truth, because he shouldn't be afraid of saying anything incorrect. But it contradicts what I remember. Monochromia, Our Great Motherland, the only country.

I don't remember. I don't *have* to remember anything here. If Iridescia did not exist, why am I here If he was not from Iridescia, why am I here She was momentarily unable to classify all these statements into two categories, true and false, black and white. There is only one category. She closed her eyes for a moment. So the other category must be false.

Monochromia, might not exist.

The word 'might' lost its uncertainty almost as soon as it was uttered in her mind. It does not exist. It does not exist! Yes, you are absolutely right, Edwin, you cannot have heard of Monochromia, because there is only one country! I am going to the only country, departing from here, departing from *nowhere.*

It was a sense of absolute assurance, more secure and reliable than any other form of persuasion or guarantee. Yet there was no expression on Fragment Number 29's face. She was not permitted to show any kind of joy; the most vivid expression should be the expression of pain and suffering, she suddenly remembered. 'Thank you, Edwin . . . I have been waiting for this answer ever since I first met you.'

'Really? I am happy to hear that,' Edwin laughed again. 'Although we have only met up once.'

Fragment Number 29 looked at him blankly. Only once? It's impossible, he must be joking. 'You really do suffer from short-term memory loss,' said Fragment Number 29 with an expressionless grin. 'Let me test your memory. Dark purple is called violet, deep blue and green makes emerald . . . do you remember telling me this?'

'What are you talking about? I have never talked about violets with you.' Edwin's voice lowered instinctively as his eyes goggled. He was not annoyed by her illogical questions, because he could see from her face that she was not playing pranks. There is always a tint of sadness in her black eyes. Whatever I say, she has never got rid of such sadness. 'I thought talking about my garden would make you feel happier, because you always look really sad.' He blushed, enhancing the pink shadow on his cheeks. 'But I didn't have the chance to have any further conversation with you. You left me.'

To make me feel happier. You are always so kind to me, Edwin. Fragment Number 29 murmured silently. Do I look sad? It is the only expression that I am *allowed* to have. Sorry if I disappointed you. Maybe I will be able to smile again, when we arrive in Iridescia.

'Edwin, I know I am not supposed to say such things, but . . .' Fragment Number 29 faltered before she could make any eye contact with Edwin again. The colour of your eyes was too brilliant, too beautiful to be related to mine. I envy you, Edwin. The closer I am with you, the more envious I become. But I am here, on my way to the only country. 'I did not *choose* to leave you . . . please, take me there, Edwin. I want to be there again. To be in Iridescia again.'

'I am sorry, Fragment Number 29, but we are already . . .'

It was an unpremeditated response, thus the most truthful response. However, Fragment Number 29 had declined to listen. Don't say anything, Edwin. I know you will, I know you will take me there. I still remember your promise. Please. Hold my hand and depart. We will be there again.

The air was no longer still. Fragment Number 29 stood tiptoe with her arms outspread, her hair flaunting in the turbulence caused by a sudden change of atmospheric pressure. The scars on her arms disappeared magically as the cloud began to dissipate; she felt that Edwin was keeping her hand in his reassuring grasp. She did not face Edwin, not even a glimpse. Her own feelings are enough to pacify any misgivings. Threads of cloud wisped before her eyes; strokes of a different colour diffused as they drifted away. It was a fragrant colour. Her body was taken over by the force of air, all her thoughts dissolving into a suspension of tranquil enjoyment. It is the true colour of the sky. She was in the sky, the sky without clouds.

'I still remember. Everything that you have said to me, the dream that we have promised to share . . . the sky is blue. This colour has a different name, which is far more beautiful. It is called *azure*. We are flying, in the azure sky.'

Tears sidled along her cheeks. She knew for sure that she was *crying*. The agonising happiness that she is experiencing now almost strangled her; her heart was overloaded with fulfilment and anxiety.

I have never forgotten. They are shards of the future, each of them is embedded deeply underneath my fingernails, and it hurts me every time I touch. Now the pain has been devolved on my heart. It is swirling and twitching, but I feel so secure in this pain. See, the wind has become milder. It must have perceived my wish. I don't want to land. I wish I could be confined in this sky forever. Let me remember more.

'Ring around the roses, a pocketful of posies.'

Fragment Number 29 whispered softly. She could not recall the source of this line, nor its real meaning. Maybe it was the phrase 'deep red' that reminded her. It did not matter anyway.

'What did you say?'

Edwin's voice was signalled by the red-tinged breeze. No, nothing. If I said anything, it would be from *your* memories.

'You know, Fragment Number 29 . . .' he hesitated, holding her hand more tightly, 'I really . . .'

He is looking at me now. Fragment Number 29 thought, I can *feel* his eyes, feel the green path of light that they have reflected upon my pupils. What are you going to say? She sensed something warm on her lips. I must not cry. I want to show you my happiness, because we are in the airspace of Iridescia.

'I really . . . like your smile, Fragment Number 29.'

She had missed out the second half of the sentence on purpose. Smile? Am I smiling? She rummaged the air to find a misty mirror, groping for the most trivial change on her face. 'Edwin, Edwin, am I really smiling?'

'Of course you are. I have never seen you smile . . . you look beautiful.'

Fragment Number 29 closed her eyes at last. I belong to this place, therefore I need not be fearful of anything. Please don't let go of my hand, because we are about to land now . . . the

70

fragrance of the flowers is much more intense here. How many flowers are there in your garden, exactly? I want you to teach me about all these colours.

'Welcome to my garden.'

We are not flying any more. Fragment Number 29 blinked, searching around nervously. Her eyes could not focus properly, until the soothing voice gently held her in his arms. She felt as if she was still in the embrace of the mist of light, because everything was soft and tender underneath her feet. An innumerable amount of gleaming spheres was freely dancing in the air; each of them had a different colour. As soon as her fingertips reached their surface, they burst into thousands of even more delicate droplets, releasing a sweet scent. They are petals enveloped in soap bubbles. Fragment Number 29 gaped at the falling petals when her vision finally became clear. They are the greetings from all these *nameless* flowers here. The garden had no hedge around it, as if its boundaries were broadening indefinitely, if it had any boundaries.

'Is my garden even more beautiful than your dream?' Edwin laughed excitedly, unable to resist the temptation of making boasts. 'All my guests are intrigued by my flowers when they enter my secret garden.'

'Secret? It can't be a secret. It is too big to be hidden,' Fragment Number 29 said without looking back, as if her eyes were fixated on the dancing petals permanently. 'But I have exactly the same feelings. It is more beautiful than my dreams. Thank you, Edwin . . . for being here with me.'

'Fragment Number 29, we are not in your dreams any more. I am showing you all my flowers in full blossom, because you are special,' Edwin whispered affectionately, his fingers swimming in her aqueous hair. 'I have never seen anybody's hair this long. Have you never had a haircut?'

'Don't change the subject, Edwin.' She leaned backwards, reposing her head on his lenient shoulder. 'What did you say? Why am I so special?'

She could feel Edwin's face flush when her palm grabbled for a smile there. 'Well, you know what I mean . . .' Edwin stuttered, 'did you say you want to know more about flowers?'

Oh, you are distracting me again. You are always like this, Edwin. Fragment Number 29 smiled, although she had not yet become used to this new privilege. She decided not to keep asking. 'Yes, flowers . . . tell me what they are called.' She held his hand actively, their fingers interlocking together. The password was shared with nobody. 'For example, the *dark red* one hanging above the bush with trailing spikes. It looks a bit frightening though.'

'Ah, you mean amaranthus? It's one of the most exotic-looking plants here. Well spotted . . . well, I suppose it's quite obvious,' Edwin said, outlining the spikes in air, 'why do you find it frightening?'

'I don't know . . . maybe it's because of the colour. Doesn't it have a more common name? I am sure it has. Amaranthus is too botanical for me to remember.' Fragment Number 29 tried to forge a relaxed voice, yet the dark red colour only became more disturbing. It looks so familiar, the dripping redness of this dark flower . . . She shook her head slightly. 'What is the "better name" for dark red?'

'It is a very good question,' stammered Edwin, 'I'll have to look it up. Anyway, shall we look at some *normal* ones? You see this one . . .' he said in a high-pitched voice, picking up a petal randomly. 'It's from amaryllis. The flowers always come in clusters, and there are many varieties to it. Although creamy white is pretty enough, I still prefer the peachy-coloured ones.'

'It's got a tender touch.' Fragment Number 29 gave up the idea of being inquisitive at last. I don't want to think about it any more. She pinched the edge of the petal carefully; a fresh smell stained her thumb. 'Doesn't it only blossom in autumn?'

'How can you say you know nothing about flowers!' Edwin grinned with an amazed look. 'Autumn is the best season for it to survive, but it's November anyway.'

'November?' Fragment Number 29 automatically raised her head. The sky was so warmly blue, and every leaf in the garden was as verdurous as the purest collection of emerald. 'I can't believe it. It is November?'

Edwin nodded confidently, selecting one more petal from the flowery cushion under his elbow.

'This tiny purple petal is from lilacs. Have you noticed the white rim around each petal? It is so skilfully done. I guarantee that even the finest brush would never be able to paint a colour as delicate as this one. By the way, they come in even denser clusters, and they usually blossom in spring.' Edwin pointed at the purple clusters, looking even more self-satisfied.

'Wait a minute. Did you say they blossom in spring?' Fragment Number 29 jumped abruptly when she received a positive answer. 'So why is the amaryllis . . .'

'It's a magic. My secret garden is a garden of all seasons, yet also a garden of no seasons. Whether November or May, my flowers never wither.' Edwin shrugged, as if it was a basic fact. 'Calm down, I didn't mean to make you jump.'

It's not scientifically realistic. Every flower will wither; every leaf will fall at some point. Fragment Number 29 gave Edwin an unconvinced glance. But it is true indeed. Everything was truly happening, right before her eyes. Flowers of two contradictory seasons were flourishing harmoniously, this was the fact that she could never deny. 'Why is it? How does it happen?'

'I said, it is a magic, a miracle.' Edwin beamed with joy, grabbing another handful of petals. 'You should know why this happened.'

'How should I know? It's my first visit to your garden . . .'

No, it is not. As Fragment Number 29 stood up,

74

she saw hundreds of fragrant fragments streaming down her white nightgown. I have come here many times, that's why I know amaryllis only blossom in autumn. You have told me all of this, Edwin. Why can't I remember? Why do I remember? Her line of sight began to meander again.

'Of course you know . . . because *you* made it happen.'

Edwin did not seem to have noticed the confusion in her eyes; he stepped forward, encircling her fragile waist in his protective arms. She instinctively slumped onto his chest. 'You are special, Fragment Number 29. Only you have the reviving power to make such miracles come true. You are my *Flora*. Do you know who she is?'

'She is the Roman Goddess of Flowers,' Fragment Number 29 muttered at a sub-conscious level. The soporific warmth from Edwin's hands was too endearing to be felt.

'I can't remember telling you this. It must be innate. Can I call you Flora from now on? It's much better than Fragment Number 29.' Edwin slowly placed his chin on her bare shoulder; a melting sensation sent a shiver down her spine. 'I have always had a single thought, since I met you for the first time . . .'

I don't deserve this name, but I love it. When is our first meeting? It must be a long, long time ago. I don't have to be a fragment any more. I am Flora now. 'I would like to . . . have a surname as well. My surname is not 29 . . .'

Deep red spikes flashed before her eyes. Is it a *reminder?* I know what I am talking about. My given name is Flora, and my surname is . . .

'Do you mind *my* surname, Flora? I *know* you like iris.' Edwin's voice rustled in the breeze, caressing every inch of her colourless skin until it was rendered pink. 'I have always been waiting for this moment, I have always wanted to do some-thing to relieve your worries, whatever they are. I want to *protect* you.'

I am not worried, Edwin. I feel so happy here, safe and secure. I would love to have a *family name,* because families do not exist in the non-existing country from which I have escaped . . . I have been taken away from my parents, and so is every-body else in that country. I don't care. It is com-pletely different now. I will stay here forever, I will have *my own identity.*

Fragment Number 29 clasped his wrist with a tearful smile. 'I would love to hear you call me Flora Iris, Edwin . . . I would love to . . .'

'Thank you, Flora. I would love to be with you forever, too.'

Forever. The very word ignited the air. Every-thing was entangled in an inevitable swirl of futur-istic remembrance, like a rewinding cassette. Forever? What does it mean?

Fragment Eleven

I will never leave you. I will never leave you *again.*
Flora Iris murmured to herself, I promise.

'This is called lily-of-the-valley. It's a spring
flower blooming in autumn, only to please you,
my Flora . . . are you listening?'

'My Flora.' This name still sounded strange,
even though it had been uttered a thousand times
since she accepted it. 'Yes, I am listening. Lily-of-
the-valley,' she said, gently holding his hand. 'I
can feel the tenderness of these white bells without touching.'

What happened yesterday was like a dream. She
became silent again as her thoughts began to
combine with the simple and elegant breath
exhaled by the lily. She found herself lying in the
garden when she woke up in the morning, not
somewhere else that she used to be. Millions of petals
in all colours and shapes decorated her nightgown, and Edwin was smiling at her. Good morning, he said. Good morning, my Flora. She could
not believe that she was not dreaming. The air,

the fragrant air, was too real to be true. And all these flowers were still blooming together, in spite of their seasons, all singing and dancing together. These colours were alive. Red, yellow, green, blue and purple, they were immortal. How little and bleak I am in comparison, she felt. I must be a blot on the landscape. I don't deserve to be accompanied by such vividness, I don't deserve to be protected by this watery blue sky. Yet she was happy. She was happy because she could be here, in her dreamlike reality.

'Do you know what it signifies?'

Oh, it's his hypnotic voice. His hands had never left her body, wherever she would go. She needed his body temperature, in order to ensure that she was alive, too. 'I don't know what it signifies. You are the expert, Edwin,' Flora Iris whispered. 'All I can remember is that I have seen it before. Not in your garden, but somewhere else with you.'

'I have specially chosen this flower to show you, because it is *our* garden now. Lily-of-the-valley signifies "return to happiness", and it's one of the most popular flowers for weddings.'

'Wedding? Don't be so prankish, Edwin. My heart is too frail to face anything that heavy. What are you making with its delicate stems? Be careful, don't hurt them. What is this feeling now? Return to happiness, have I returned to happiness? If I have never experienced happiness, how can I decide whether it has been *returned* to me?'

Flora Iris quivered when the third finger of her

left hand threaded through the greenly woven ring of sweetness and poignancy. The latter soon prevailed, washing away all the other emotions. The white bells blended into a fine mist as they liquefied and streamed down, then crystallised at her feet. A strange woman was frozen in the crystal. The woman was holding a bouquet of lilies-of-the-valley in her arms, wearing a snow-white wedding dress. Petals rained down from the bouquet like tears, yet the smile on her face was calm and sincere. Somehow, the fallen petals generated an atmosphere of tragic serenity around her. Flora Iris noticed a ringlet drooping over her right shoulder. Her hair was purely black, too, but slightly curly. Flora Iris looked up to her with admiration. She is so beautiful. She is in her own world, under the shelter of the crystal. I have seen her somewhere, Flora Iris finally recognised. I remember seeing her . . . in Edwin's garden, with all the flowers and colours in the air. Who is this woman? Her appearance indicates that she is from Monochromia *as well*, but there is only one country! She cannot be from nowhere, unless she is an illusion . . .

Flora Iris could not divert her gaze from the woman. 'Who are you?' she murmured nervously. 'I like your white dress . . . have I ever met you?'

There was no answer; the woman's smile was still sweet and peaceful, the petals still tender and pure. However, the cold radiance circulating inside the crystal had never changed. She was staring at the outside world without any focus, as if she had no control over her own expressions.

'The blue one here is a bit fragile. Its petals are so vulnerable that you would feel guilty for your life if you broke them. It has a beautiful name, though. Forget-me-not,' Edwin continued, without realising her wandering away from him.

'Forget-me-not. Who have you forgotten? Who have forgotten you? Please, talk to me. I know it's not very comfortable if somebody you don't know keeps talking to you . . . but somehow, somehow I feel that you are someone I can confide in. So, can you listen to me? Please?' Flora Iris began to panic for apparently no reason; the unbreakable surface of the crystal echoed her own voice. Nothing had changed, yet she could not follow her own thoughts any more. This woman, she thought, this woman is meant to be someone important. Very, very important . . .

Flora Iris moved closer, holding her hands together. 'Are you from Monochromia, too? You seem very happy, because you are smiling . . . but I know you feel deeply, deeply sad inside. Can you tell me why?' She smiled with difficulty. 'Oh, sorry, you don't have to tell me anything . . . but I am really happy here. I have eventually arrived at the place that I have been longing for all my life. I belong here, although nothing here belongs to me. And somebody loves me here!' Flora Iris glanced back; nobody was behind her, yet she didn't seem to have paid any attention. She continued with some kind of excitement. 'My true love is for Iridescia itself, but my love for *him* is also true. I cannot afford to lose him . . . I hope he will understand one day, I dare not tell him now . . . I don't want to hurt him.'

Edwin's eyes narrowed with suspicion. He was standing next to her, carefully listening to her unilateral conversation with a non-existent image in the air, observing the slightest change in her emotions. He finally decided not to interrupt.

'Fragment Number 29, you shouldn't talk to that woman when someone you love is watching you . . . he will be *jealous* of her, if you keep treating him with neglect. But there is nothing unexpected. Your behaviour is totally predictable and understandable, because *I* made it happen.'

Everybody had left the meeting room, except the professor. The crystalline coating on the white screen echoed her monotonous voice. Her eyes became unnaturally moistened with a tiny drop of an aqueous irritant as she moved towards the screen; a silvery reflection flickered on her spectacles.

'Fragment Number 29, you must remember . . . I am a Victorious Fragment, not Number Nil any more.' She sneered at her own shadow plotted on the unfathomable screen, rubbing her gloved hands against each other. It is already November, no wonder it's so cold here. 'How many years have

I spent in this cold place? I was *nothing* when I first came. I still remember what they said to me on that day. Do you want to become *we*? Cooperate with us if you do. And they succeeded. The research here could not have begun without my contribution. The Great Calibration would never have succeeded with such efficiency if I had not become *we*. I shall be very proud.'

'In the name of Guardian M, Our Great Leader,' The professor mumbled in her loving voice, touching her forehead with three of her gloved fingers. She could detect no temperature there, so she put down her hand with a disappointed sigh. 'My gloves are ever so white. No contamination has ever occurred here, apart from one incidence.'

'What are you going to dream about next time, Fragment Number 29? Do you really think that you are Flora Iris now? Yes, you are Flora Iris, but you are also Fragment Number 29. You cannot escape, Fragment Number 29, never. I don't want you to worry about anything. You will be safe and secure *here*, I am looking after you. Even if I have the ability to destroy everything in your brain without effort, I will not do it. You have to help me, help me to remember. Then I will cleanse, and refill you.'

'Now . . . enough of this stupid soliloquy. Would you mind if I shared your dream with you? I am sure you wouldn't.' She laughed scornfully; her eyes were still adhered to the shadow, as if she could ferret out somebody else's face. 'Because you cannot dream without me.'

Flora Iris had a dream last night. It was a dark dream. Everything she loved was gone, and she was forced to leave her dream. A voice was calling her name there, the sweet voice of a strange woman. She was wearing a white wedding dress, a bouquet of lilies-of-the-valley wept as she broke down before my eyes.

She did not smile. Flora Iris saw tears rolling down her cheeks. Dark, dark red tears trickled down from her colourless chin like flower spikes. My blood is not black! The woman shouted at her with extreme pain and fear, but she could not see anything black there. It was the most elegant and sincere form of red. Don't be afraid, it is a beautiful colour. She told her soundlessly, it has a better name that I can't remember any more.

You made me bleed. You made my blood turn black . . . but it was my own choice. I was willing to sacrifice everything for you . . .

The bouquet fell down; blood-stained petals flew everywhere. The woman did not scream. Remember, she sighed faintly. Remember that your happiness will not last very long here, or anywhere. You must remember . . . you will never belong to this place.

Her entire body melted down after she left her last message. The white wedding dress was immediately drenched by a mixture of dark red and black liquids, pouring out from somewhere secret in her heart. Her lonely ringlet was floating on the meniscus of the tranquil liquid. Flora Iris gasped as the liquid reached her ankles, her waist, and her shoulders. A suffocating smell of rust engulfed all her senses; everything she inhaled was nauseously clammy and corrosive. She did not know where she was, and she did not want to know. It could not have happened in Iridescia. The only country should be a country of absolute happiness and freedom.

'Do I have the right to possess the happiness and freedom in Iridescia? My own thoughts stifled my powerless wishes. No, don't lock me up in such darkness. I have escaped, I have escaped from it! No! No! I will not let my love drown, I will not be called a Fragment again!'

'You have to face the reality, *my little Flora* . . . I am sorry, I am very sorry . . .'

The woman's feeble cry faded into the red infinity; a new, yet similar voice soon replaced hers.

'Everything you have is everything you have *here*. Nothing else exists. Nothing else will ever exist.' The abysmal valley of sombre sweetness rippled when a drop of syrupy voice landed heavily. The voice was no longer strange. '*We* granted you happiness and freedom, as a single fragment. Don't forget, you are still monochromic. You can-not change the fact.'

'It is not the fact! I am here, and nobody can force me to leave! Nobody! Nobody!'

Flora Iris cried in futile resistance. 'Only Edwin could rescue me. Where are you, Edwin? Please, help me see the reality. Tell me this is not the fact! The fact is that I am here with you, and nothing else! Tell me, Edwin. Please! Please . . .'

'And you woke up at midnight.'

Edwin Iris placed another wet towel on her forehead. 'My Flora, I was so worried about you . . . I thought you had a fever.'

Have I been muttering in my dream again? Flora Iris opened her eyes in fatigue. Sorry, Edwin. I am always a nuisance. 'Where am I now?'

'You are in *our* bedroom. Do you not remember?' Edwin grinned uneasily. 'I don't know what you dreamed of . . . anyway, are you feeling any better? You have not talked to me for nearly a day.'

'Have I been sleeping all day? I am so sorry, Edwin . . . but it is so nice to see you here again,' Flora Iris whispered sorrowfully. 'Are you really here, Edwin? Am I still in Iridescia?'

The duvet had some kind of pale patterns on it. Flowers again . . . how well I know you, Edwin. Orchids and magnolias this time. I wish I could smell them. Flora Iris sat up slowly. She saw her own reflection in the mirror, obscured by a hazy beam of light. Edwin was in the mirror with her. Even the mirror image was so faithful; his emerald eyes and blond hair dimmed because of her *illness*.

'I am sorry, Edwin. I don't know why I am like this . . . I really didn't mean to trouble you.'

'Oh, my Flora, please don't apologise. I have promised that I will protect you, even in your dreams,' Edwin said with an involuntary sigh. 'What made you feel this sad? Who was forcing you to leave?'

She felt something bitter surging over her eyelids. It is not red or black, it is transparent. 'No, Edwin . . . let me keep it as a harmless secret.' Her voice was comforted by the transparency of her tears; she stared at the icy droplets on her insentient hands, as if she was waiting for a colour change. 'You will not believe me anyway . . . because you are an Iridescian. You have never experienced any nightmare, you are always so happy.' She smiled ironically. 'Of course you should be happy. I would be happy to die if I . . . if I . . . had ever belonged to this country.'

'What are you talking about, my Flora?' cried Edwin, 'What happened in your dreams? Whatever you say, I will trust you! Yes, I am happy, because everything I have is here! I want to make you feel happy as well, even happier than I am!'

'But why? It's not your duty! Why are you so kind to me? Why do you want to make me happy? Why? Why did you take care of me? Why did you bring all these colours to me? Why did you help me to escape?!' Flora Iris shrieked hysterically; more tears shattered on her hands, like falling shards from a broken necklace. 'You know I don't deserve all these! You know these things have never belonged to me! You know, you know . . . I am not Iridescian . . .'

'Does it matter?! You are here with me, safe and secure,' Edwin clutched her wrists carefully. 'Why is it so important to you? My Flora, I will never be happy if I cannot bring happiness to you! I don't care where you come from, I don't care who is chasing after you! I want to make you feel happy because *I love you*!'

'See, you cannot understand what I meant. You don't know how it feels.' Flora Iris took a deep breath as she began to realise her emotional turbulence. 'I don't want you to be involved. Edwin, I am serious. If *they* ever found out that I am in Iridescia, they would destroy us without hesitation.'

'How? Who is this "they"? Why would they destroy us?'

'You find it shocking, don't you? You don't believe me, Edwin. I will not tell you who they are. They are our enemies, it's a battle that we can never win. They are from nowhere. I am from nowhere.' Flora Iris gazed at him, calmly and softly. 'What I see is the fact. Nobody can change the fact. You are here, close to me. Will we still be here? As long as we are still in Iridescia, we will be here *forever*. Nobody has the power to expel me from this country. I am from another country, Edwin. I was so happy when you told me that you have never heard of it.' Flora Iris held out her hand. Once again, she needed his body temperature for her own existence. 'Edwin, have you ever ... have you ever met another woman like me before?'

'Another woman like you? In what aspect?' Edwin frowned, yet such expression was soon inhibited by another smile.

'A woman with semi-long black hair, but slightly curly. She had a bizarre ringlet hanging from her right temple.' Darkness infiltrated her hollow eyes as she uttered the sentence word by word. He had already said no in her mind.

'No ... I don't remember. Perhaps you are the only woman in Iridescia who has black hair.' Edwin fondled her fringe with a bemused look. 'You are unique, my Flora.'

'Am I really?' Flora Iris turned her head to the mirror. 'Am I really the only woman with black hair in Iridescia? No, I can't be, I can't be!' The reflection on the mirror quivered and tarnished, as if the mirror itself was to smash. 'Should I be happy? Should I be happy to be unique? No! I don't want to be different *here*! I want to become *we*, I want to be one of *us*!'

'Flora, my Flora, why are you crying again? Did I hurt you? Tell me, tell me what have I done wrong!' Edwin embraced her. 'Oh, my dear Flora, you must have been suffering in your dreams. What can I do to make you happy, my Flora?'

Flora Iris did not answer. Suddenly she held Edwin in her arms with all her strength, until their breath could eventually amalgamate into a frail thread of fatal affinity. I love you too, Edwin. Please, make me yours, she muttered silently, Make me *colourful.*

Fragment Twelve

'This is disgusting!' a man in black uniform yelled. 'How can you let her do this, professor? It is *disgusting*!'

'Now you know why she was sent to the Centre at the age of eleven.' The professor shrugged, staring at the screen with contempt. 'Can you believe this? She has been dreaming for ten years. Our special project only began three years ago, in order to make her *feel better*. We were too busy to do anything about her before that.'

'I would feel sick if I were her,' replied the man. 'Is it one of her privileges in the Centre?'

'Oh yes, of course. You know, we cannot destroy anything without creating it first. Just like the fact that trust is the only shortcut to betrayal.' The professor smiled approvingly. 'We will utilise her trust in that man. He is not what he appears to be, remember. She thinks that this – as you can see on the screen – is the only method to prove such trust. Her body is simply a donation.'

'But what will this donation produce?' The man

grimaced, with his black hands half-covering his eyes, as if he was an eyewitness to the most inhumane crime scene. 'Professor, I really . . . look at her! Look at the colour . . .' his voice descended in nervousness, 'the colour . . . of her face.'

The professor smiled proudly, yet secretly. She enjoyed observing the colour displayed on this man's orthodox cheeks. You look even younger than Fragment Number 29, she thought. When were you released from your collective nurturing facility? The black uniform you are wearing cannot help you to be less immature. You have exactly the same colour, why are you not ashamed of it? 'Do you know what it's called?'

'I . . . I don't know. It is neither black nor white.'

Liar. She scoffed at the man's deceptive cautiousness. This colour is inside your blood vessels, you little sycophant. 'Can you see this top button?' she held up the remote control to the screen, 'What colour is it?'

The young man's lips shuddered, inadvertently forming a bloodless R. No sound was uttered, no word was pronounced; the letter R hit his darkly polished boots with a thud. The professor had no intention to move her eyes away from him.

'I said . . . it is neither black nor white. It is the colour . . . of Fragment Number 29's face.' The man stepped back as the professor approached even closer. 'I don't know what the name is . . . am I, am I supposed to know?'

'No, you are not supposed to know. You don't know anything before I tell you,' she said, carefully wiping the black case of the apparatus with her white cuff. 'You are perfectly right, it is neither black nor white. It is *red*, as you can remember yourself, it is a *red* button.'

The monosyllabic word *red* frightened him. He was struck by the appalling simplicity of this word, yet he was too afraid to dispute. The professor replaced the remote control. You do have an interesting expression. Aren't you aware that this sort of expression is forbidden as well? Are you shocked? I will be very disappointed if you are not. 'A single red button does not necessarily make the Centre itself polychromic.' She patted the man's shoulder to stop it quivering; a shadow expelled the last trace of her gentleness as she continued. 'Nothing does. You have to have complete trust in your own monochromic nature. If you think that this button is black, it is black. Nobody can change or erase its blackness. Monochromism is not what is reflected upon your eyes, but what the reflection *becomes* when you see it. You did hear me say that word, yet you could have chosen not to hear it.'

'Sorry, professor! I am sorry, I really shouldn't . . .' the young man shrieked in fear when the professor paused. 'I shouldn't have chosen to see it! It's black, professor, it's black!'

'It has become black, I hope.' She stroked his head, calmly whispering, 'Don't worry, everybody makes mistakes. The *black* button on the remote control is merely a test, and you have done well. You are a promising young Fragment, thus you must understand the reason and meaning of being monochromic.' Her silver-rimmed spectacles shone with satisfaction. 'How I wish Fragment Number 29 was as hopeful as you!'

The man sobbed, rubbing his eyes hastily with his black gloves. 'Thank you, professor. Somehow I wish I was sent here at the age of six as well. My calibration did not last very long . . . I didn't even get a chance to talk to you, professor.'

'The shorter the process lasts, the more successful it is.' The professor adjusted the brightness of the screen; Fragment Number 29 had ceased her actions. She was panting, her hair flowing all over her lover's bare chest. 'The calibration of Fragment Number 29 has persisted for years, which is not helpful at all. That's why we will use a different strategy when she wakes up this time.'

'This time?'

'Yes. This is her last dream. She has been awakened several times by physiotherapy – it's my colleagues' idea. Does it sound any better?' She laughed. 'In fact, we have been delivering these dreams into her mind, so as to enable us to terminate her dreams whenever necessary – this time, eternally.'

'Does it mean the success of her calibration?' The young man's eyes brimmed over with curiosity. He was no longer frightened; the fascination of having a *private* discussion about The Great

Calibration with his honoured professor had excited him to the highest energy level.

'The Great Calibration had been a total success already,' said the professor. 'We will not calibrate Fragment Number 29. We will . . .'

Her insidious smile dispersed in the air. To him it seemed to be the ultimate encouragement, as if it was part of his duty to facilitate the process. 'Refill her?' He jumped feverishly. 'Are we going to refill her?'

'After her final dream, yes.' The professor gazed at him in delight. 'I was not as keen as you are now, when I was at your age. Perhaps you can do something for us when you have completed your training.'

'Professor, I . . .' He stuttered; the bright sweetness of her voice heightened the glorious darkness in his eyes. 'I . . . I would love to, but . . . I don't deserve this, professor. I am . . . inexperienced.'

'It is your advantage nonetheless, because . . .' the professor stopped abruptly. 'I think everybody else is coming soon, but no worries. It is a private conversation.'

'I don't want to disrupt your meeting.' the young man said uneasily.

She checked the doorway again before she resumed. 'You wouldn't be able to disrupt *our* meeting even if you wanted to. As I was saying, being inexperienced is good for you. It means that you are more likely to make fewer mistakes.'

Moreover, whatever you do, don't accept the

offer of being the inspector for the Centre. The professor clenched her white fists; she decided not to go any further.

The screen flickered, switching to a different channel automatically. A girl in white blouse and white skirt gradually came into view. Somebody else was behind her, casting a white shadow at her white feet. It was a feminine shadow.

'Are we there yet?' the girl asked feebly in her undeveloped voice, 'is it our new facility?'

'No, it is not our collective nurturing facility,' replied the shadow, keeping the defenceless hand of the little girl in her greedy grasp. '*You* will be transferred to somewhere else.'

They were walking together on a black footpath. Nothing could be seen around them, apart from the fine mist drifting under the black sky like white cotton fibres soaked in ink. What has my tutor just said? You, instead of we? Her hand perspired in despair. What will happen to me?

'Where is this place?' the girl blubbered, 'if it's not our new facility, where is it? What does the place do?'

'Shut up, Number 29! We are sending you there because we want to help you!' the shadow roared scornfully, pounding her feet in anger. 'The place will take our responsibility for you. You don't want to go back to where you were yesterday, do you? Just shut up, otherwise you will end up in the Re-education Committee!'

Yesterday. What did I see yesterday? I attended

a public lecture, and there was a woman on the stage ... cables was connected to her limbs, because she was deleted ... she was to be deleted ...

The last phrase silenced the girl; an unexpected onset of dizziness made the air tremble. Dark red spikes dribbled down from a dazzling white background.

Fragment Thirteen

Number 29 had eventually reached the end of the road. Her tutor had led her to the entrance of a white building, a building that was almost invisible in the mist. Only the black barbed wire could remind her of the hidden existence of the building; this time, it had left no trace on her white skirt. She could hardly distinguish between the gate and the whitely tiled wall. The mist was cold. She was standing at one of the six corners of this snowy hexagon without a single movement, as if she knew that somebody would come to put a warm blanket on her shivering shoulders. There was nothing else in the entire area; in fact, even her tutor was ignorant of what sort of area it was. Is it still a part of the Capital? All she could remember was walking, and continue to walk until her legs became numb with muscle cramp. She could not see the full picture, yet the serenity and grandeur of the building was intriguing. Despite her usual fear of the uncertain, it was a beautiful place. It was the first time that she found beauty outside her collective nurturing facility, even though there was no explanation for the origin of such beauty. She was ready to be assimilated into the snowflake without any reason.

The shadow behind her was silent. Her tutor was slightly disappointed by Number 29's reactions; she expected it to be another chance to reinforce her power over the girl. Silence continued to prevail until the gate squeaked quietly. Another white shadow emerged from the mist.

'Stand still, Number 29!' her tutor yelled in a voice full of respect and adulation when Number 29 tilted her head instinctively. 'You are always a defiant number, no wonder you can never become a Fragment!'

'She will, my compatriot. That's why she is here.'

The second shadow squatted down to stroke Number 29's hair. Nothing is more suitable for this beautiful place, except this sweet voice. Number 29 narrowed her eyes. The woman's hand had a silky touch, but it was a bit cold for her.

'Do you want a new name? I know, nobody likes to be a number. You should be different from everybody else.'

A young woman's face unveiled as the mist slowly faded away. I hear the forbidden words, *I* and *different*. Number 29 gaped at her in joyful astonishment. She looked beautiful, too. Have I ever met her before? Her beauty is so affably familiar.

'Professor, she is . . .' Her tutor gasped, 'why did you . . .'

'You don't tell *me* what to do!' With the sweet smile still shining on her face, the woman muffled Number 29's tutor by a simple gesture. 'Has she always treated you like this?'

Number 29 nodded, decisively and thankfully. She did not know where her courage came from, yet it was certain that this woman would protect her.

'They are envious of your uniqueness.' The woman took Number 29's hand tenderly, giving her tutor a sullen glance. 'From today, she is Fragment Number 29.'

'But, professor, she has not been calibrated yet,' her tutor grumbled secretly, 'she is the victim of her parents' childhood neglect, and it is already too late for her to be educated . . .'

'Are you deaf? Do you want me to send another memorandum to the central office of your facility, saying that you have been arguing with me?' The woman stared at her tutor with an even stronger signal of disparagement. 'She does not need calibration. She has become a fragment without being calibrated – is it clear enough to you?'

Number 29 did not look back. You are on my side! She sobbed excitedly, I don't have to be afraid of telling the truth, the gloomy shadow is not behind me any more! 'Who are you?' she asked in undertone, 'what is . . . your number?'

'I am not a number,' grinned the woman, 'I am a Victorious Fragment. Just call me professor, like all my colleagues do.'

Professor? Is it your name . . . no, I mean, your number? But you said you are not a number. You must be unique as well. The woman's maternal smile became more and more familiar; Number 29 was sure that this could not be their first meeting. She was determined to find out later. 'So, professor . . . where is this place? What are we going to do here?'

'Here is your new home. I am sorry, I have left you waiting in the cold.' The professor stood up. 'I will tell you everything in a minute. Shall we go in, Fragment Number 29?'

Fragment Number 29's heart fluttered; her new name sounded melodious because it was given by her only guardian and mentor. The professor winked at her former tutor before pressing a series of numbers on the combination lock, but she paid attention to none of these acts. I can forget everything about the facility, she thought, I am not one of them. 'Fragment Number 29,' she murmured when they started to stride along a boundless corridor; the dazzling whiteness almost disorientated her. 'It is my new identity.'

'You don't have any identity,' the professor laughed quietly, 'you are a Fragment of Monochromia, Our Great Motherland.' Her unreachable figure swiftly moved from one corridor to another like a silver bead rolling in a white labyrinth, allowing Fragment Number 29 no chance to look behind.

'A fragment,' Fragment Number 29 repeated curiously. 'Yes, I do remember ... some of the numbers from my facility are called fragments as well.'

'Oh, forget about it. You are here, you are different,' replied the professor. 'Now you are a part of the Centre.'

'The Centre?' Another new term.

'Are you wondering where this place is, and what we do here?' The professor stopped; everything (if there was anything) in the corridor stiffened like a film negative. 'This place is where I work as a scientist. More precisely, a forensic psychiatrist. Our mission is to convert unhappy numbers into happy fragments, and we have discovered the best way of achieving it.'

'Am I an unhappy number? But I am a fragment now.' Fragment Number 29 blinked with a bemused look.

'You are special. For example, you remember too much,' the professor explained didactically. 'Remembrance is the inception of all unhappiness. Guardian M, Our Great Leader, wants all of his glorious citizens to be happy. Therefore, we must not remember. Everything you have is everything you have *here*. Nothing else exists. Nothing else will ever exist.'

'Being monochromic is being happy. Being oblivious is being happy.'

Fragment Number 29 muttered subconsciously. It is definitely not our first meeting, professor. She raised her head, I remember you saying the same thing to me, word by word. I remember your elegant posture, your carefully arranged hair, and the calm smile on your face ... nothing has changed *since then*. 'Why am I here? I am not unhappy. Why am I here?'

'Fragment Number 29? Have you remembered something, Fragment Number 29?'

'What have I done?' The focus of her pupils staggered; she nestled up to the professor, helplessly and anxiously. Are you talking to me, professor? I feel really dizzy. Your white arms are ever so warm to me, just like the warmth of ... Her field of vision blurred, as if she was peeking through two hazy membranes adhered to her eyeballs. 'I am sorry ... perhaps that's why they could not deal with my *illness* any more.'

'What have you remembered, Fragment Number 29?' asked the professor. 'Can you hear me?'

Just like the warmth of the red liquid on your hand.

Silence. The screen darkened; the image was automatically frozen at a programmed moment.

'This is the beginning of Fragment Number 29's incessant dreaming, isn't it, professor?'

A blank-eyed man pointed at the screen. The scientists assembled again in the meeting room; the young man in black uniform winced as everybody else stepped in. 'What exactly did she remember?'

'Our first meeting,' the professor replied. 'We first met in the year before the official deletion of her parents. My compatriot, I believe that nobody in the Centre actually predicted such reactions. She fainted even before I took her to Room Ai!'

'Ah, she somehow broke into the Re-education Committee to take part in the lecture. I do remember that,' another male scientist said proudly.

'Of course you do. You were standing right next to me, whinging that I had not saved you a seat.' Somebody else interrupted in a tranquil yet powerful voice, 'I am surprised that she did not recall the lecture straight away.'

'I am not sure if she ever did. Maybe she will do later,' the professor snickered, 'You must be itching to see the impact of the first lecture, as the former lecturer of the Committee. However, I am afraid that we will terminate her dream soon. Eternally.'

'Eventually,' the former lecturer grunted.

'It is a shame that you were unable to participate in our observation – or distortion, rather – of Fragment Number 29's memories. She has reunited with her ideological lover.' The professor shrugged again, looking at him pitifully. 'Ideology is the synonym for *thought* . . . a logical thought cannot exist without a correct ideology. Perhaps you would like to know what had really happened to her.'

'Only if I need to know.'

'We all need to know. In fact, she is pregnant. We impregnated her.' The professor halted for a while to follow the highly amusing expression displayed on the former lecturer's face. She coughed lightly. 'My compatriot, do you remember our friendly chat about haemoglobin?'

Fragment Fourteen

Amaryllis, lilac, lily-of-the-valley and forget-me-not. Red, purple, white and blue. I have not forgotten everything. Nothing has ever faded away since last November. Now it is September again. Have I been here for too long? It must be a dream.

Flora Iris stroked Edwin's blond hair. Will my baby have the same hair colour? She smiled.

'What are you laughing at? Is there any food on my face?' grinned Edwin, resting his head on her lustrous lap. 'Keep your voice down, our daughter is sleeping.'

'How can you tell?' Her laughter became even louder. 'What if he is a boy? He is kicking around all the time.'

'Girls are more active.' Edwin curled up to her pregnant stomach. 'I can hear her talking to me.'

Flora Iris squinted at him. 'She must be grumbling about you disrupting her sweet dreams,' she tapped his forehead, 'Have you decided her name yet?'

'Well, I will call her Little Flora.'

'So what about our second daughter? Little Little Flora?'

Edwin looked up. 'Don't be so greedy, my Flora. Five is just about enough.'

'Oh, stop jesting with me!' Flora Iris complained, 'I am serious. Let me think . . . a girl's name beginning with an F. I might need your help.'

'Fluffy.' Edwin jumped away dramatically, his face reddening with excitement and pleasure. 'Or Feathery? How about Flying?' He spread out his arms, as if he was preparing for taking off. Petals flitted up and down at his feet like kaleidoscopic streamers.

I must be dreaming. Flora Iris carefully held out her hand to collect the falling petals. Every day here was like a dream, a dream in which she could indulge herself in all these colours. She had never imagined that the colourfulness of her dream would persist until today. But she was still here, in Iridescia. It is too late for anybody to wake her up, so it cannot be a dream. 'Edwin,' she whispered to the rosy bud sprouting in her own body, 'Thank you, Edwin.'

Here is *our* secret garden, a garden of all seasons. The petals evaporated from her palms, suspending in the air like volatile droplets in a condenser. These droplets gradually formed an aromatic cloud. It is also a garden of no seasons; I can conjure up flowers in every colour, whenever I wish. I am his Flora. Flora Iris lowered her head, evading the sparkling tenderness of the cloud. I have experienced all seasons, in this secret garden of no seasons. Spring is as lively as phloxes, pink and delicate. I would like to sit with him on our flowery blanket, waiting for a cup of camomile tea to infuse. Summer is dazzling and vigorous, like clusters of yellow forsythia. I would like to saunter around the green countryside with a chiffon parasol, waiting for him to find me and bring me home. Autumn is like love-in-a-mist. It is reminiscent of my first meeting with him, deep and genuine. I would like to knit him a pair of purple woollen gloves, keeping him warm day and night. Winter is cold and bleak, yet full of hope and expectation for the next spring. Tuberoses are the emissaries of winter. They will parachute from the cloudy sky, and melt into teary dews at my fingertips. I would like to decorate the ground with our white footprints, and my breath will entwine his heart with all my love.

A thin layer of moisture obscured her field of vision. The sensation was too real to be imaginary. She loved the scenery here; it would make her shadow glitter with colour. Perhaps it could not change the blackness of her eyes, but it had granted her the right to appreciate all these colours. It had granted her the right to be happy.

'Everything I have is everything I have here. When I wait for the unforeseeable twilight to arrive, when I long for the intangible clouds to descend, I shall freeze the scenery forever. I am so happy that I am still here, until this very moment.' Her hands slid down her watery cheeks tentatively; she realised that she was weeping.

Why, it shouldn't be painful. I am here, together with everything that I love. I have no regret. But why? Why am I still scared?

'Edwin,' she began to cry. 'Help me, Edwin! Please, don't make me leave, don't let them take me away! I can't leave this country, I haven't even come up with a name for my daughter!'

Crimson tears trickled down from her face. It tainted her white nightgown, gradually forming an irregular ellipse. Everything was silent, as if they had been imprisoned in a monotonic photograph. A pungent odour clung to the petals, remorselessly bleaching away their colours. They streamed down in black and white liquids, decaying and disappearing.

'Edwin! Edwin! Where are you?! Our flowers, our flowers are dying!!' Flora Iris screamed, distraught with terror. 'What's happening? Help me! Edwin!'

Another onset of pain plunged her into the writhing sea of withered petals; something warm and viscous flooded out between her legs, accumulating into an array of red spikes. She attempted to wipe off the liquid, yet her body was no longer in her control. 'Edwin! Where are you?!' Her voice became hoarse. 'I will ... our daughter will ...'

'This flower with dark red spikes is called *Amar-*

anthus caudatus. Don't you think that its botanical name sounds much better?'

A sweetly gloomy voice congealed the spikes. 'Have you got a good name yet?'

'Edwin . . . I know my illness is incurable, but . . . I am afraid . . .' Flora Iris murmured frailly; her consciousness was drifting away with the red liquid. 'This time . . . perhaps I cannot recover . . .'

'So, what is your daughter's name?' the voice insisted. 'A name beginning with an F?'

Flora Iris closed her eyes in fatigue. 'My daughter. Edwin, did you hear it? Your dream has come true. Call her . . . Felicity, please. Felicity. It's a beautiful name. Where is she? Why can't I see my daughter?'

'Because her name is not correct,' interrupted the voice. 'I have a brilliant name for you, beginning with an F.'

'No, I will not change my mind. My daughter's name is Felicity, Felicity Iris.'

'Are you sure?' The voice lowered itself, as if it was disappointed.

'Who are you? Who's talking to me?' Flora Iris quivered, still unable to stop the flow of the red liquid. 'Are you here, Edwin? Edwin?'

'He will not help you. He is not what he is!' the voice laughed satirically. 'I can't believe that you have forgotten who I am. It's time to come back, Fragment Number 29!'

The frozen photograph rattled, and disintegrated into millions of crystalline grinds. It was far more vulnerable than she had imagined, so fragile that even a disturbance of air could destroy it.

'No!! I am not Fragment Number 29! I am Flora Iris!' she cried fanatically, 'I am not going back! You cannot take me anywhere!'

'You are absolutely right, Fragment Number 29. We cannot take you anywhere, because you are coming from nowhere,' the voice sniggered. 'You are coming back to us. Only we can protect you, Fragment Number 29. Only we can grant you eternal happiness. Your daughter does not exist. She is nothing, not even a Fragment.'

'No! Give her back to me! Edwin! Edwin! Help me! Tell them I am not Fragment Number 29! I am your Flora, tell them, Edwin!'

Nothing was visible, nothing was accessible to mitigate her pain. Every word she pronounced was another impulse of agony. 'Edwin did not help me. Edwin had left me!' she screeched in despair, 'Please! Let me see him again! Please! I want to know who he really is!'

The red liquid spattered onto a horizon of infinite darkness, suppressing her last breath with its stifling sweetness. Whatever it takes, I want to meet you again. Edwin! How can I not love you, Edwin? And Felicity, how can I leave my daughter without having heard her first cry?

'There is only one way.'

Fragment Number 29 was unable to recognise the voice, but its soothing and healing power had revealed its identity. 'There is only one way to meet up again, my Flora. Then you will find out who I am.'

'You are Edwin, Edwin Iris! I promise, I will come back to you, to Iridescia! Wait for me, Edwin. Please!' Her tears dissolved in the red liquid, smoothly generating a murky solution. 'And then . . . I will be . . . Iri . . .'

'Bring another colour, my Flora. Bring another colour to *Monochromia*, and I will be with you again.'

The omnipresent darkness had at last vanished. A feeble rhyme echoed in the empty atmosphere:

'Ring around the roses, a pocketful of posies.'

Fragment Number 29 uttered the words without knowing their meanings. She woke up.

Fragment Fifteen

A fragmented mirror in Room Ai gleamed insidiously; its role was not to present the accurate reflection of an object, but to distort it. The mirror image of Fragment Number 29 became a jigsaw puzzle made of irregular geometric shapes, yet none of them was separated. She could hardly figure out if she was facing the mirror directly. She was encompassed by its shards, and there was scarcely any free space for her to move around. Millions of light beams interlaced and intersected with one another; their explosive energy almost blinded her.

Fragment Number 29 squinted, trying to focus on the thin gap between two contiguous fragments. She eventually found a relatively stable image of herself there. Her arms were spread wide, stiffly, as if they had been nailed onto the wall with silvery swords; her shabby nightgown was unable to conceal the black scars on her forearms. She struggled to unlock her arms, but a burning sensation forced her brain to transmit signals to her nerves. She groaned.

'Where am I? What has happened?' Fragment Number 29 moaned faintly. 'Why am I here?' She looked up with difficulty, as if she was waiting for an answer to descend from the ceiling. The ceiling was a mirror, too. She saw her own eyes half-hidden in her murky and lifeless hair, like two black pearls covered in seaweed. I have lost something, she noticed. Something has been taken away from me. 'I can't remember,' she said to herself nervously. 'Something important has gone, but I can't remember.'

All of the duplicates of her mirror image stared at her nonchalantly; their predatory eyes frightened Fragment Number 29, although she knew that she was the creator of the black hole in her own pupils. But there was no escape. These reflections blended into a monochromic hologram, outlining the misty figure of a woman in white.

Fragment Number 29 recognised her. Without her bouquet, the smile on her face became unstable and unnatural. Her arms were covered by her white satin dress, yet the penetrating light in the room revealed the black shades underneath. 'I cannot help you any more,' the woman said with poignant serenity. 'I cannot keep our promise. I am sorry, my little . . .'

It was the only message from her. The image evanesced into the colourless air, before Fragment Number 29 could cling to the last trace of it. 'Help me,' she quivered motionlessly, 'anybody . . . help me, please!'

'You are not in danger, Fragment Number 29. You are in our protection.'

Suddenly, a sweet voice pierced her eardrum. It was not the same voice, yet mysteriously similar. Perhaps I misheard it, she thought, There is only one voice.

And she had always thought in the same way. Everything affiliated to this voice was long-waited. Fragment Number 29 shook her head, as if she could not believe that there was another person in the room. 'Where are you? Are you here to help me?' She cried in irrational gratitude, 'Please, take me out of this place. I shouldn't be here . . . somebody else is waiting for me!'

'Why shouldn't you be here? Why are you so scared? You are not alone, Fragment Number 29. You are with me here, safe and secure.' The voice became closer and closer; she could even perceive its approaching footsteps, without knowing the exact direction. She felt as if the voice was walking around her, instead of towards her. 'Do you remember me? I would feel sad if you don't, because I am your caregiver. You wouldn't have come back here safely without me.'

The owner of the voice strutted out of the glass wall; it was a woman in a white coat. Her alluring beauty stunned Fragment Number 29 instantly. I love your smile, Fragment Number 29 stuttered silently. I feel ashamed of myself when I look at you. 'Who are you?' she asked impatiently, 'Are you my . . .'

'I am your protector.' The woman smiled; her lips shone with warmth and tenderness, as if they were coated in white honey. She was now standing in front of Fragment Number 29, displacing her flimsy reflection with an authoritative yet feminine figure. 'You have been suffering from a continual nightmare,' the woman petted her pallid cheeks with a sympathetic sigh, 'but now you don't have to worry any more. We have rescued you from the nightmare.'

'A nightmare? Maybe ... I think ... I was having a painful dream,' Fragment Number 29 mumbled in a trembling voice, 'Yes, it was painful ... really painful. The most important thing in my life has been taken away, and I ... I couldn't do anything to stop it.'

'Tell me,' the woman questioned in an even softer tone, 'what have you seen in your dream? Where have you been?'

'I don't know ... I can't recall any details. All I remember is a place with many, many flowers ... they all had different colours, and ... I met ...'

'Do you know where you are now?' The woman frowned, her face darkened with dissatisfaction. 'You are not dreaming any more, remember! Tell me where you think you are.'

Fragment Number 29 could not reply. Even the question itself sounded so familiar that no assumptions could be made to counteract such familiarity. She gazed at the woman in fear and respect. She is wearing her hair in a chignon, Fragment

Number 29 noticed. Perhaps I can do the same myself . . . I am sure my hair is longer than hers. No, it will not work. I must not imitate her, because she is my . . .

'You are a real challenge to my patience, Fragment Number 29. Shall I tell you the answer?' shrugged the woman. 'Maybe it will help you to recollect the truth. How happy you are . . . at least you can pretend that you've forgotten everything.'

I am not pretending. Fragment Number 29 argued secretly, I am not lying. I have never remembered the truth, the capacity of my long-term memory has been deprived of unwittingly. So please tell me where I am. Tell me *where we are.*

The woman winked at her. 'We are in Monochromia, Our Great Motherland. There is only one country, and there will only be one country,' she said blankly. 'Fortunately you will not dream any more. The colours in your nightmare will no longer bother you – they have never existed.'

'Monochromia? Did you say, I am in Monochromia?'

Fragment Number 29 screeched. Monochromia. This word was more than enough to squeeze her empty, banishing all her thoughts and anticipations. Monochromia. A country that she had risked her life to escape from. 'No . . . this can't be true . . . I am not . . . I am not . . .' she stammered in trepidation. This woman, this mercilessly amiable woman . . . who is she? She knows everything about me, who is she?

116

'I am a Victorious Fragment,' the woman introduced herself proudly. 'Just call me professor, like
all my colleagues do.'

'Professor . . . ah!'

The woman clutched Fragment Number 29's
throat without forewarning; her gloved grip tightened and tightened, as if she would fill up her
lungs with vacuum. 'You have just committed a
crime, Fragment Number 29. A CRIME!' She sniggered, exclaiming in undertone, 'Traitor.
Insurgent.'

'No . . . please, don't . . .' Fragment Number 29
scrabbled for air, although her arms were
restrained from making the most trivial movement. She could see no chains or shackles; it was
the power of air that fettered her. 'It should be
Monochromia, Our Great Motherland . . . but
why? Why am I here? I should be in . . .'

'It's too late to take it back,' the professor said,
coldly loosening her grasp. 'However, maybe it's
still possible to expiate your crime.'

'I will do whatever you want . . . please, don't
kill me . . .' Fragment Number 29's cry sank down
into an inarticulate whimper; she dared not look
at her contorted reflection in the mirror. She is
the professor, she is a psychiatrist in the Centre
. . . She intermitted her recollection with a sharp
intake of breath. 'Please . . . ah . . . I can't . . .
breathe . . . please . . .'

'We are facing a national crisis.' The professor
lowered her voice. 'Monochromia, Our Great

Motherland, is at war with another country. A *non-existing* country.'

'Iridescia!' Fragment Number 29 screamed instinctively; she was shocked by the raucousness of her own voice. 'It's Iridescia! Iridescia is at war with Monochromia, Our . . . our . . .' Immediately she realised that her dreams were not fake. I cannot say it. Monochromia is *not* . . . yes, I can remember now. I was in Iridescia! 'It does exist!' Fragment Number 29 panted helplessly as the professor contracted her grip again, 'Iridescia does exist . . . what do you mean? What do you mean by . . . *at war?*'

'The infallible stability of Monochromia, Our Great Motherland, is under threat. Our country needs your help, Fragment Number 29. And it is your duty to offer your help with the highest pride and glory.' The professor continued with a solemn face, 'The purpose of your dream is to infiltrate Iridescia, the non-existing country. You have performed the task very well, but it cannot succeed without intervention from the Centre.'

It was not a nightmare. It was the sweetest dream I have ever had. I don't believe you! You are working for the Centre, for *the opposition*! 'No, it's not true . . .' Fragment Number 29 whined fraily, 'Iridescia is the country where I met . . . Iridescia is the country of . . . colours . . .'

'Are you sure?' A sinister grin appeared on the professor's face. She let go of her hand abruptly, pressing Fragment Number 29's abdomen with

118

professional precision. 'Here. Don't you feel that something is missing here? This is what Iridescia has done for you.'

Fragment Number 29 did not gasp for air; even her eyelids began to shiver. Something has gone, taken away from my own body. The most important thing in my life has gone. Tears cumulated in her eyes. 'Professor ... Now I have nothing to lose. Everything I loved ... is gone.'

'No, it is not gone yet,' the professor sneered compassionately, 'we are here for you. We want you to be happy, Fragment Number 29.'

'Happiness is not the only thing that matters. I want to know the truth,' Fragment Number 29 sobbed, 'the reality. Being happy is less important ... I want to know the reality.'

'Being happy *is* the most important thing, Fragment Number 29. Your happiness affects our happiness; therefore, we must ensure that you are always happy.' The professor inclined her head, holding Fragment Number 29 in her benevolently rigid arms. 'To infiltrate Iridescia,' she murmured, 'so that every one of us will be happy.'

Fragment Number 29 blushed palely, intrigued by the professor's composure. She had not been embraced by anybody for a long time; her amorphous antipathy to the professor disintegrated like a melting cube of ice. 'Why is my happiness so important?'

The professor raised her head slightly; an inscrutable smile replaced her seriousness.

'Because you are the last one to be refilled.' Her fingers crept onto Fragment Number 29's wilted lips, sincerely and coercively. 'Don't underestimate the importance of *your* happiness. You made Monochromia, Our Great Motherland, at war with Iridescia. Of course, Iridescia does not exist; but such non-existence had induced a negative effect on the *conformity* of your happiness.'

'Sorry, professor . . . I am confused. Could you please . . . unlock my wrists? They really hurt,' Fragment Number 29 pleaded in embarrassment, 'I can't think properly.'

'Unlock? What do you mean? Nobody has locked you up.' The professor stared at her with surprise. Fragment Number 29's body fell down from the glass wall with a sharp and metallic crack, as if the invisible shackles on her wrists were shattered by the professor's lenitive voice. An unprecedented sense of total relaxation anaesthetised her brain. She placed her hand on the professor's shoulder with timid gratitude.

'I am so scared,' Fragment Number 29 cried, moistening the professor's white epaulette with her cloudy tears. 'Every cell in my body hurts, yet I don't know why . . . I could not move my arms, I could not control my own body.'

'It is because one of your cells is malfunctioning.' The professor knelt down, softly stroking Fragment Number 29's cheeks, 'It's an error in the system. Every cell should work collectively under a single guideline, otherwise your body will suffer.' The movement of her hand slowed down. 'Monochromia, Our Great Motherland, is like a functioning body. We, as her glorious citizens, are the building blocks of the body. If one of us became unhappy, the entire body would be unhappy. Although one malfunctioning cell can never destroy the system on its own, it will inevitably affect the overall productivity and stability of the system. You feel unhappy, don't you? You feel painful, don't you? I know you do, because you are the malfunctioning cell.'

'Is this why . . . you are going to refill me?' Fragment Number 29 asked in fear.

'Exactly. You are very clever, Fragment Number 29.'

'Why didn't you do it earlier? You don't have to wait until now. You could have done it ten years earlier!' Fragment Number 29 exclaimed, holding the professor with even more *passion*. 'Why did I have to go though all these dreams? Why did I have to lose everything, after having experienced all the happiness . . . in Iridescia?'

'The central dogma of refilling is to expose, not to terminate. You will never be able to realise the reality if you have never dreamt; you will never be able to recognise sadness if you have never been happy.' The professor fondled her hair. 'However, even the happiness in your dreams has its own nationality. You said you were having a painful dream in Iridescia. Why do you think that it was *happy*?'

121

'I don't know ... I can't remember, I can't remember! Please, don't force me to remember anything ... I can't! What do you want from me? I can't...' Fragment Number 29 cried in short breath, 'If I am the malfunctioning cell ... why don't you dispose of me?'

'I have never said that we will not dispose of you. Missing one or two negligible fragments causes no adverse effect,' the professor explained quietly. 'But it cannot bring us victory. We must not annihilate the malfunctioning cell without having conditioned and *repaired* it first. We need your memories, Fragment Number 29. Our country needs your memories, because only you have successfully penetrated Iridescia.'

'I did not mean to penetrate Iridescia. I was happy there ... before I woke up.' Fragment Number 29 shook her head. 'I never had any other purpose. I just ... I just wanted to be happy! I just wanted to forget ... about everything ...'

'To forget about everything that happened in The Great Calibration? Don't worry, we will not calibrate you. Please trust me, Fragment Number 29. I have been doing this research project on your illness for three years, and that was *after* The Great Calibration. You see, our purpose is the same as yours. Guardian M, Our Great Leader, wants all fragments to be happy. Our country wants you to be happy,' sighed the professor. 'The happiness that you experienced in Iridescia is disguised misery, in essence. Happiness is nation-specific, even though there is only one nation. The so-called happiness in Iridescia . . . is the ultimate horror in Monochromia, Our Great Motherland. You can feel it yourself, because you are the victim of it.'

Fragment Number 29 hesitated. It cannot be the correct explanation, yet nothing could be more credible. She took a deep breath. *He* did not come when I cried for help. He did not come. 'I am sorry, professor . . . sorry for being an anomaly in your research. My illness is incurable. Just eliminate me, and everything shall come to an end.'

'You are not an anomaly. Nothing can be done in the Centre without you, Fragment Number 29. You are the subject, the most precious sample.' The professor smiled. 'Don't be so pessimistic. We will refill you with the reality, as you have requested. We will return the reality to you – and, in exchange, we need your memories. Undistorted memories.'

Undistorted? Fragment Number 29 frowned in deeper confusion. Everything that has happened so far is distorted? What is this *everything*? She looked up; her mirror image shown on the ceiling was still fragmented and unreal, as if she did not have a solid form. I am no longer innocent. Have I ever been innocent? She smiled bitterly, I am a criminal, an insurgent, a traitor. My blood is polychromic. Yes, I can still see it. When it dribbled down like dark red flower-spikes, I was stained polychromic. When the first couple of deleted numbers was favoured with Guardian M's amnesty, I was stained polychromic. They were granted the privilege of being polychromic until the last second of their lives, because I saw them bleed. Red, red spikes were blooming zealously. Fragment Number 29 gave the professor a listless glance. What did they say when they were officially deleted? Their deletion was too efficient to be observed in details; I have forgotten *their* perception of perpetual forgetting.

'Don't you want to go back to Iridescia, to resume your *mission* for us?' The professor asked in a lulling tone, gently pressing down Fragment Number 29's head onto her lap. 'I promise that everything you see this time will be the truth. However, please bear in mind that everything you remember will be used *against* Iridescia, our greatest enemy. You will remain fully conscious in this process.' She put her right hand in a pocket inside her white coat, ensuring that her movement was indiscernible to Fragment Number 29. 'Now, close your eyes. We will help you to recall the *correct* reality.'

'The reality can exist in illusions, just like illusions in the reality. They are not self-contradictory. Similarly, you can be consciously aware that you have fallen into unconsciousness.' Fragment Number 29 followed the instruction with great care, 'Iridescia only exists because I have never left Monochromia; it's not in my control as to how they will use my memories, *but*...' Suddenly her eyelids convulsed open; transparent tears rolled down her face with a prickling sensation.

'What's wrong? Why are you crying again?' The professor's voice stayed unchanged, as if everything was as she had predicted. 'There is nothing to worry about. We are helping each other, Fragment Number 29. My colleagues and I have been waiting for this moment for *twelve* years . . . don't disappoint us.'

'Will it be painful, professor? Will the refilling process be painful?' Fragment Number 29 whimpered. 'Please, don't make me suffer any more. Please!'

The professor pulled out her hand cautiously. 'We have never made you suffer, and we will not. Iridescia has. It is the fear of the uncertainty, the non-existing entity. Just relax, Fragment Number 29. It is a highly enjoyable process.'

'So why? Why am I . . . so sad? Why do I still suffer . . . from this pain?' Fragment Number 29 clutched her neck, as if she was to be choked by her own emotions. Why? This sudden burst of pain . . . when I agreed to assist the Centre . . . when I agreed that Iridescia *is* the enemy . . .

'No more tears, no more. All you need to do is to invite us to your terminal cycle of illusions . . . in order to *reconstruct* the reality.' The professor muffled Fragment Number 29's lips with a loving look, dropping down something spherical from her artful fingertips.

Fragment Sixteen

The gentle touch of the professor's white glove gradually weakened as her fingertips left Fragment Number 29's lips; even her body temperature began to fade away, becoming more and more distant from her. Fragment Number 29's head drooped helplessly, holding out her hand towards the professor. Don't leave me alone. She whined in silence, Where are you going? Don't leave me.

'I am always with you.'

Fragment Number 29 could clearly hear the professor's smile, although her voice was misty and volatile. She crouched in a corner, searching for a reflection of the professor's white shadow on the parade of broken mirrors.

Professor! Where are you, professor? Fragment Number 29 cried in fear, yet she was unable to sit up or do anything with her own body. She felt something slippery sliding down her throat; it soon entered her bloodstream, desensitising and stiffening her unprotected erythrocytes. Where are you, where are you? Even the professor has abandoned me! Her images, distorted and shattered images, blended into the glistening fume released from the glassy walls. She saw her watery eyes melting down like two spheres of black ice. The black liquid flowed over her cheeks, staining everything in its dark pathway.

'It is not a painful process,' Fragment Number 29 wheezed, 'if I close my eyes, I will see the truth. Now I have nobody to rely on, so let this black liquid flood the room.'

'You must have been very lonely. I know how it feels, especially when you cannot trust anybody else but yourself.' The professor finally appeared behind Fragment Number 29; she knelt down and held her left hand.

Fragment Number 29 shivered as the white tenderness of the professor's glove touched her fingertips. The soothing smell of the fume dissolved and filtered the black liquid, quietly comforting her disturbed mind. 'Professor? Are you talking to me? You have come back for me?' she whispered. 'I have been . . . I have been . . .'

'Waiting for me here?' The professor smiled, slightly inclining towards Fragment Number 29, 'But I have never left you. You must remember, I am always here for you. Whatever you are going through, we will go through it with you.'

'So what am I going through now? I can't see you anywhere. Everything is white, the white clouds, the white light coming from the ceiling . . .' Fragment Number 29 sobbed in anxiety,

'I have been . . . dreaming, haven't I? Everything in front of me is merely a dream, aren't they? Why can't I see anything?'

'Because you are crying. Your own tears blurred your field of vision,' said the professor, supporting Fragment Number 29 to sit up. 'You are not dreaming any more. You are now travelling with me, towards the *reality*. Let me wipe your tears away.' The professor caressed Fragment Number 29's face and sighed. 'It must have been very lonely, being in a cold room like this for ten years. But you really don't have to sit on the floor. What if you hurt yourself with these sharp pieces of glass?'

'Perhaps I would be very happy,' replied Fragment Number 29 in a less nervous voice, 'as you said, professor . . . I have been very lonely, and I always will be. So . . .' She lifted her arms, looking surprised of her own movements. The numbness inside her body had dissipated, and her hazy reflection on the floor had become clear. 'Look, professor,' she leaned forward and pointed at the glass shards, 'these mirrors have once my only company. They will never hurt me, no matter how close I am to them. Even if they did . . . even if they tore me apart, I would still be very happy, because at least I could feel some kind of intimacy from it. At least . . .' Her voice once again became frail; she hesitated until she received an approving look from the professor. 'At least, I would know for sure what had been inside me . . . what I had always remembered.'

'It's not what you are really thinking of,' the professor said, carefully coiling a lock of Fragment Number 29's hair around her index finger. 'But I will not ask you any questions. I am being totally truthful with you, Fragment Number 29. Now we are working together, we are going to the same place. Only two of us. Therefore, I trust you, Fragment Number 29, in the same way that you have always trusted me.'

I trust you. This long-waited phrase tightened Fragment Number 29's chest, as if her heart had been elevated to its flash point. She grasped the professor's wrist, staring at her feet. Her entangled hair half-covered her legs, softly shading her white nightgown with black stripes. She had lied, she had not been fully truthful to her only caregiver. Why? It is unnecessary to be afraid of telling the truth, because she is trustworthy. Fragment Number 29 thought, giving the professor a guilty glimpse.

'Here is Room Ai, a room of your very own. Why are you afraid of it? Why are you afraid of me?' asked the professor, with a forgiving smile. 'Your reactions remind me of something that I have long forgotten.'

Fragment Number 29 tilted her head nervously. She stretched out her left hand, cautiously stirring the threads of dense fume circulating in the white air. 'Are we there yet? Have we arrived yet?' she murmured. 'What will we see behind the cloudy air?'

'Are you looking forward to seeing it?' said the professor. 'I am sure you are expecting something special to come, something different . . . just like me.' She leaned back and crossed her arms, as if she was trying to hide a gift box from a curious child. 'I was expecting the same thing. Something new, something different. But I was terribly wrong.'

'You *were?* When?' Fragment Number 29 moved even closer.

'I like the way you emphasise the words. That's exactly what brings up my memories.' The professor laughed quietly. 'Before The Great Calibration, I was always expecting *something* to change. During the early years of Monochromia, Our Great Motherland – from 2023 to 2028 in particular – people had too much freedom. Being over-creative or over-constructive is even worse than being rationally destructive, Fragment Number 29. It must be difficult for you to imagine, those five years of instability and non-conformity. People could go on the streets to promote their own opinions about the governing party, and wear silly rosettes for the most disastrous form of social turbulence, the so-called process of *election*. Unfortunately, none of them had realised the fundamental fact that there was only one party, one society, one country.'

The professor shrugged with disappointment. She glanced at Fragment Number 29, and continued. 'In year 2027, when I was doing my second doctorate at the Institute of Psychiatry of the Capital University, there had been a book-selling activity in the campus shop. A woman was signing her new book. Again, it was the most detrimental form of documentation, because the content of the book was fictional. She even gave out free copies to the students, the unwitting victims of thought pollution.'

'But you were there, too. You were . . . one of the students who asked for her signature.'

Fragment Number 29 mumbled, looking at the ceiling with a blank face. Every word from the professor had become a pixel of a larger picture, projected onto the glass wall in the shape of an irregular geometric object. There was no sound, no motion, but she knew the storyline. She saw a young woman in a purple suit, showing a white-covered book to someone else. A blue rosette with red stripes was pinned onto her collar.

'I have always loved her book,' she said to the other person, 'it's especially useful before the election.'

'Useful? Why?' asked a man's voice, his face remained unseen. 'Don't mix up fiction with reality. The oppositional party is already declining, and you are still supporting it! Do you really think that the election will take place? I don't want you to become one of those liberal lunatics.'

'Of course it will take place, and I will vote for the minority!' she argued, 'because there must be an opposition. Otherwise . . .'

The picture froze, and suddenly disappeared. A sharp intake of breath interrupted Fragment Number 29's thoughts, as she began to receive more words from the professor. She blinked, and looked down reluctantly.

'Luckily, such negative actions and speech had never worked. All those people, who had once believed in the existence of a second country, were soon proved completely wrong by the construction of the black sky. It was a rather tedious process. The project took eleven years to complete, followed by The Great Calibration, but we have eventually achieved total stability, in spite of its time-consuming nature. Differentiation causes nothing but anxiety, doubt and unhappiness. People are easily frightened by their own imaginwation. They imagine themselves to be free individuals, and they start getting paranoid about everything. Our Centre used to specialise in forensic psychiatry, especially the assessment and treatment of delusional disorders.'

'He used to work in the Centre, didn't he?' Fragment Number 29 asked abruptly, 'because he had always admired you, even though you held different opinions.'

'Who? It is such an illogical question.' The professor frowned with suspicion.

'The man you were talking to at the book fair.'

'I didn't talk to anybody there,' The professor replied with a calm smile. She clasped her hands, gazing at Fragment Number 29 without showing a trace of uncertainty. 'Why did you say that?'

Fragment Number 29 said in an almost undetectable voice. 'Because I can remember your purple suit, and the blue rosette.'

'Remember? You were born in 2031, the year in which I first joined the Centre,' laughed the professor, 'how could you remember anything before you were born?'

'I was born in 2031?' Fragment Number 29 looked away.

'Don't you trust me? How would I ever, ever use those forbidden words?'

The word *forbidden* muffled Fragment Number 29's thoughts. 'Sorry, professor,' her voice began to panic, 'I didn't mean to offend you. I just felt as if I had always remembered something . . .'

'I am not offended at all,' said the professor, gently patting the back of Fragment Number 29's head, 'we all remember things. Some of them are correct, some are not. We are helping you to remember the correct things.'

Fragment Number 29 stuttered. 'So these memories must be from somebody else. Somebody else must have told me something . . .'

'Let's get rid of all the uncertainties in your speech,' the professor interrupted, 'your false

133

memories are from nobody, but yourself. That's why you cannot think logically. Your mental disorder must be cured, the sooner the better.'

Mental disorder? Is remembrance a kind of mental disorder? Fragment Number 29 looked at the professor in confusion; her eyes watered as the white fume in the other end of the room started to fade away. Somehow she was afraid of the clarity behind the clouds. 'Whatever it is,' she whispered, 'you said you would go through it with me.'

The professor slowly stood up. 'Don't be so pessimistic, Fragment Number 29. No matter what it is, the present or the past . . . they are the episodes of a short film. We should feel proud that we are now able to record all these episodes, and process them when necessary.'

Fragment Seventeen

The white clouds dispersed, exposing a liquid crystal screen behind it. It was specially designed and installed for an untitled episode, ready to be viewed in Room Ai. Fragment Number 29 could hardly believe that she was still at the same place; she felt as if the images were expanding, its *colourful* resolution power amplifying at an exponential level.

'It has always been colourful, hasn't it?' asked the professor. 'Come closer and tell me what you think.'

Fragment Number 29 did not make any movement. She gazed at the screen; a stinging sensation clung to her lips as she heard the word *colourful*. Monochromism is not what is reflected upon your eyes, but what the reflection *becomes* when you see it. 'What can I see now?' she murmured. 'If what I see here is true, everything else will be false. Is everything colourful outside this room, outside the Centre?' She looked up to the professor, her face turning even paler with a constant sense of foreboding. Yet she received no answer. The bright light in the room had enhanced the clarity of the enormous screen in front of her, until nothing else was left in the room to obscure her vision. The condensed residue of white fumes, almost intangible under their foamy disguise, encapsulated the shattered mirrors.

'Professor . . .' Fragment Number 29 moaned, trying hard to resist the instinct of shutting her eyes. 'Perhaps I will be ill again, after seeing this you will help me, won't you? If I have another *onset* of . . .'

'Why are you so afraid of your own mind? Isn't this a long awaited moment for you, Fragment Number 29? After ten years of solitude and despair, isn't this what you want to find out the most?' replied the professor. 'Of course, things are different outside this room, outside the Centre. People enjoy their daily benefits from Monochromism, which is unshakably dominant in every aspect of their lives. They have the right to sustain freedom, because they can see no colours, not like you. You are the statistical infrequency.'

Fragment Number 29 nodded with a faint smile. 'So nothing is colourful outside the Centre. Here is the only place where I can appreciate all the colours that I remember.'

'Yes, appreciate. Appreciate your own remembrance, plus the fear of it.' The professor laughed softly.

Fear and appreciation, pride and guilt. They

are like the intersection point of my hands. Fragment Number 29 thought, loosening her grasp from the professor. Unlike the fragile imagery projected on the ceiling by herself, the translucent screen generated pictures with multi-sensual precision and realism. The first image displayed on the screen was a woman wearing checked cotton gloves and a pink apron. She had black eyes, and a ringlet dangled above her right shoulder. She was holding a metallic tray, with some yellow and blue objects with an apparently soggy texture lined up on it.

Fragment Number 29 struggled to focus her eyes before she could finally recognise the background. It was somebody's garden. Amaryllis, forsythia, flowering cherry and the clusters of lilac. Sunlight highlighted their delicate petals, almost rendering them transparent. The colours were so vivid and sincere; their unprocessed fragrance instantaneous captured all her sensations. Red, orange, magenta and mauve, everything was incredibly harmonious. Nobody would believe that such beauty was created by electrical currents. Fragment Number 29 leaned forward, carefully holding up her hands to touch the screen. The liquid crystal rippled, but the integrity and quality of the image remained unaffected. It is real, she secretly spoke to herself, Everything I see here is real.

The woman walked forward, placed the tray on a wooden table and took off her gloves. 'Mitchell,' a sweet voice vibrated in the air, 'would you like some fruit cakes?'

'I am on a diet,' answered a man's voice, 'but I'd love to have them all!'

He sat on a deck chair and picked up one of the puffy things from the table; the golden frame of his spectacles shone as he swallowed the cake and smiled. He was wearing a navy blue shirt and dark grey denim trousers, forming a clear contrast with the woman's pinky clothes. Fruitcakes with coloured icing? Fragment Number 29 stared at him, wondering what kind of pleasure he could get from eating food colourings. His face reminded her of another man, although he had completely different features. The similarities possibly did not come from his appearance alone. The woman looked at him with great affection; colours glittered in their monochromic eyes. 'Where is Felicity?' She sat down and whispered to the man named Mitchell, 'Has she finished her painting yet?'

'Probably she's doing it upstairs,' said Mitchell. 'She said she will show it to you later.'

'Felicity is always good at choosing the correct colour. Sometimes I am not sure if this is really an advantage for her.' The woman sighed, lifting the lid of a porcelain teapot on the table. 'Mitchell, somehow I feel that something worse will happen soon.'

'What's wrong? Nothing bad has happened, my dear Irene. You are getting more and more mistrustful these days.' Mitchell gave her a reassuring glance and gently stroked her hair. 'I understand how disappointed you are about your last book being censored, but it was nothing personal.'

'I know I am not the only *sufferer*,' said Irene, pouring out a pale yellow liquid from the teapot into a glazed cup. 'I didn't mean the censorship. To be honest, I had lost all my hope after the proposal for universal suffrage ended in total fiasco. I can hardly imagine anything worse than that, yet still . . .'

'Oh, that was almost twelve years ago!' Mitchell interrupted, 'perhaps we have stayed too long *there*. You should adapt you to the social norms of *this* country if you really want to settle down and lead a normal and happy life.'

'Perhaps we should never have come back here in the first place,' Irene said quietly. 'At least, we came back to the wrong place at the wrong time. I thought Felicity would have a better future. She shouldn't have been born here. What if one day we are told to send her to one of those Collective Nurturing Facilities? What if one day we are no longer allowed to go anywhere?'

'You are paranoid,' said Mitchell, grabbing another piece of fruit cake, 'is your persecution complex acting up again? It is not compulsory to send your children to those facilities, even though it's becoming a very popular option for parents to do so.'

'It is not compulsory *yet*.' She moved closer to

him, holding the teacup towards his lips. A thread of white vapour ascended from the cup, tinted with the calming warmness of chamomile. She smiled at him with less passion, yet more confidence. 'I wish I could be as optimistic as you, Mitchell. I am sorry if I make you feel worried for me again.'

'It is not your fault, dear.' Mitchell embraced her; the yellow liquid spilled out as her hand quivered. Black sadness congealed in her eyes. 'We are here together, safe and secure. Nothing has ever changed in our house. Felicity is still staying at home, and we can still sit in the garden and have a cup of tea.'

'But we cannot be writers any more. They are trying out every single possible measure to constrain our creativity, depriving us of the basic right of appreciating the world outside Monochromia. Mitchell, I will never give up trying. I want to finish the novel I am writing at the moment, before they completely destroy our sky of free thought.' She looked up to the sky helplessly. All she could see was a turquoise canvas, bleached by an invisible barrier of optical fibres, painfully fighting with the forceful application of distorted colours. The pure whiteness of the clouds seemed deceptive and insidious.

Mitchell frowned with dissatisfaction. 'Darling, I am sorry, but you must be more considerate.' He took a sip from the teacup. 'The government is building up an artificial sky because of the increase of ultraviolet radiation and carbon dioxide levels. It is our protection!'

'No, it is *their* insecurity. They are not any safer than us. Their party exists in perpetual insecurity and fear, fear of people like us,' Irene said with cautiousness and pride, 'because we are the oppositional force.'

'There is no oppositional force, unfortunately,' returned Mitchell, 'the party members are a lot less confident, compared with you. But please remember, they are the ones in power, we are not.'

'The pen in my hand is my power. Even if it will never be published and understood by the masses, somebody will remember me. Felicity will remember me.'

'Mummy! Mummy! I've done it, I've done it!'

A little girl flew out from the backdoor, waving a piece of watercolour paper in her hand. She wore her hair in two plaits, with roseate ribbons and purple hairpins. The bright sunshine added a reddish tone to her black hair; the silvery buttons on her aqua satin blouse glimmered, together with the organza lining of her skirt. Irene stood up and cuddled her, even though the shadow of apprehension on her face had not yet disappeared.

'Look, mummy, this is my own garden!' the girl giggled with excitement. 'I put all my favourite flowers on it!' She pointed at the picture, inadvertently smudging the colours with her fingertip. 'Rose, cherry blossom, marigold, daffodil, cam-

141

panula, tuberose, love-in-a-mist...' she took a deep breath, 'forget-me-not and iris. Iris is my real favourite!'

'Well done, Felicity. I am so proud of you!' Irene kissed the little girl's forehead, 'I am amazed that you can remember so many flowers.'

'And their colours, hundreds of colours!' Mitchell clapped his hands. 'Felicity, we've made you some fruitcakes! What is your favourite colour for the icing? Yellow or blue?'

'Blue, I love blue, Blue is the colour of the sky, blue is the colour of mummy's favourite dress,' said Felicity, running towards the table. 'Mummy, daddy, can I have my own garden when I grow up? I will plant all the flowers, I will make it even more beautiful than the picture.'

Mitchell wrapped up a cake in soft tissue, and put it on Felicity's palm. 'Different flowers blossom in different seasons, Felicity.'

'It does not matter,' Felicity beamed with delight, 'my garden will be a garden of every season.'

'Felicity...' Irene whispered, and looked away. The watery blue sky, and a garden of every season. And a colourful world of happiness and freedom. You will remember, Felicity, you will remember. She thought, glancing at the red spikes drooping down from the fence. They were neglected in Felicity's painting.

Fragment Eighteen

'Have you read today's newspaper, Irene?'

Irene switched off the printer as Mitchell entered the living room with a glass of blended fruit juice. She detected a fake smile on his face. 'No,' said Irene, 'what's the matter? I've been busy writing for the whole morning.'

Mitchell glanced at the printer uneasily. 'Nothing too bad, Irene.' He put the glass on her desk. 'You haven't had any breakfast yet. I thought you might like to have some fruit juice.'

'Don't change the subject, Mitchell. Something has happened, I can tell from your face.' Irene opened up the printer, pretending to behave casually. A drop of black ink leaked from the ink cartridge when she tried to remove it, staining her hand with murky viscosity.

'We'll have a meeting tomorrow, in the Local Community's Committee,' Mitchell shrugged, 'about our new sky.'

'The Local Community's Committee,' laughed Irene, 'what a creative use of alliteration. They have finally managed to complete that project. Is the meeting compulsory? What will they do if I don't attend?'

'Apparently, everybody has to be there as punctually as possible,' said Mitchell. 'Irene, it won't do you any harm if you just go there and listen to them. I'm sure it's not going to last very long. We have had so many meetings in the last three months.'

'Yes, and now they've reached the final stage, the utilisation of *their* black sky.' Irene looked away as her voice lowered involuntarily; she could only see the sky through the gap between the half-closed curtains, yet its blue transparency still penetrated the window pane and arrived in her field of vision. It was already December, and the fine layer of frost had frozen at the intersection point between the sky and the air inside. Pale sunlight refracted through the window at a restricted angle, struggling to defend its own space. How many barriers are there, from the real sky to my eyes? She thought, staring at the lilac tassels drooping from the corduroy curtains. Is it protection, or isolation that keeps us safe and happy? No, I am neither safe nor happy. She reached for the last printout from her laptop, her fingers sliding down the page with ambivalence and regret. The glass glittered behind her, projecting a brittle highlight on her black chignon.

'This is the ending of my last novel,' Irene resumed after a long pause, 'I hope Felicity will remember it. I have been reading all the chapters to her, apart from the last one. Perhaps she's expecting a happy ending, but I'm sure there is something that she can add to it herself.'

'It has been a long time since *my* last book,' Mitchell said, gently placing his hands on her shoulders. The frail texture of her linen jacket gave him a cold touch.

Irene gave him a pitiful look, yet with a trace of understanding. She grasped his hand. 'What can we do?' She leaned back. 'What if we are the only people who remember? Will anybody remember us?'

The background trembled and shattered, as she bent over towards her desk with a deep sigh. The curtains melted down, the furniture disfigured and the carpet discoloured by the flowing streams of black and white liquids. They climbed up to the wall, marching towards the ceiling with strict discipline. The living room was being transformed to a place where hundreds of people gathered, all of them wearing white overalls with black scarves – except Irene. They were sitting in the Local Community's Committee, secretly holding each other's hands. Irene looked around anxiously, searching for a sign of familiarity. Her colourful garments seemed particularly peculiar and defiant amongst the crowd; even Mitchell had agreed to wear a creamy white suit, instead of his favourite navy blue. The chandelier in the house had been replaced by light tubes arranged in a uniform pattern, and the folding chairs had become rows of polypropylene stalls. Irene shivered when more people crammed into the room.

The brightness of illumination suddenly intensified, before the black gates of the Committee slammed close behind them. The crowd immediately became quiet.

'This is not a meeting, Mitchell, this is . . .' Irene clutched Mitchell's wrist; a resentful glare from the back muffled her.

'Stand up, please.'

A strange man's voice blasted out from the ceiling, sending its commands before anybody could recognise its origin. Everybody stood up with catatonic conformity and respect; Irene frowned, yet unable to resist the sound waves coming from high above. All she could see was the nonchalant shadows of the residents living in the same Community with her, her distant acquaintances. She wondered how it could ever have been a coincidence, that all of them displayed such stilted similarities?

'My compatriots!' the invisible man continued with enthusiasm, 'we have all come here today to celebrate the completion of our new sky, our ultimate protection and our unconquerable shelter. It will begin to function in five minutes, but there is something even more significant to come. There are thousands of Communities across Monochromia, Our Great Motherland, and every single one of them is exactly the same as ours. We are going through exactly the same process, at exactly the same time.'

There was a short period of silence, as if it was specially devised for the people to contemplate the meaningfulness of his speech. 'We shall be very proud of the political and social reforms that we have achieved since 2028, under the correct guidance of Guardian M, Our Great Leader. From today, our new sky will come into being. From today, we will be totally protected from any danger, and prevent any danger from emerging, because we will . . .'

'Implement the unique ideology, Monochromism, for Our Great Motherland.'

Another man's voice entered the room, with an even more powerful and possessive quality. The two voices mingled together, producing an atmosphere of infallible severity and superiority. Irene felt her heart pounding with intense apprehension. She had heard the second voice before. Guardian M? It was the name of the leader of the governing party when Monochromia was founded in 2023. She remembered listening to him on the news, yet she had never got used to that name. Nobody had ever seen his face. 'We are guarded by the uncertain, the unpredictable tempers of one man?' she mumbled, 'and there's only one party?'

'Please, just shut up, Irene!' Mitchell whispered nervously.

'Our new sky will ensure the integrity of Monochromia, Our Great Motherland. *My* glorious citizens, from today, we shall perform our duties with more faith and passion. We shall devote ourselves to the idea of the utmost importance. The One Country Principle, which will come into force as soon as our new sky illuminates itself. From today, individual difference will be an invalid term. From today, only black and white, and the shades of grey in between, will be permitted to exist and flourish. From today, Monochromia, Our Great Motherland, will become the only civilised country in the entire universe.'

An overwhelming sensation of confusion and disbelief stroke Irene's mind. She felt as if there was something wedged in her throat, something corrosive yet inescapable. She was thrilled by the exhibition of extreme narcissism in the man's speech, and its almost subconscious nature of aggression. The moment of realisation was accompanied by the cessation of the circulation of air. The particles stiffened and broke apart, when she heard the humming noise from the sky. The clouds screamed in anguish, as they were torn to shreds by an all-consuming force of black illumination.

Black, white, and shades of grey in between the two ends of the light spectrum. Nothing else exists. Nothing else will ever exist.

'So the sky *became* black at that moment.'

Fragment Number 29 whispered to the screen; the image froze when she diverted her line of sight towards the professor. The film footage stopped at a close-up of the black sky, taken from a specific perspective. It looked as if it was from Irene's standpoint, because she could recognise the fading lines of dark red dripping down from the ceiling as the artificial sky closed in. Then all the colours disappeared, leaving her gazing at the solitary sky with a traumatised smile.

'Where is her daughter Felicity? Is she in the house on her own?' Fragment Number 29 quivered as the thought of the little girl in satin blouse flashed through her mind. 'It must be very frightening for her, why didn't her parents take her to the meeting?'

The professor squatted down and embraced her from the back. 'What do you think?' she asked quietly, 'do you reckon that she would love to have witnessed the process of blue sky becoming black?'

'But at least she wouldn't have been left alone. Perhaps . . .' Fragment Number 29 clung to the professor and covered her ears instinctively. She heard the girl cry for help, for someone to endure this dark moment with her, but nobody came. In spite of the screen itself, her own projection re-emerged from nowhere, creating a blurred image suspended in front of her. She saw Felicity scream, crouching behind the door in her own room, with one hand clasping the hem of her skirt. It was seen from an observer's perspective, yet Fragment Number 29 was able to perceive the most trivial shift in her emotional experiences.

She could almost feel the electrical signals in her brain being gradually synchronised with those of the little girl.

'What's wrong, Fragment Number 29? Look at the screen. What are you thinking of?' said the professor. 'I'm here, don't be afraid.'

'She is trying to remember. She wants to remember . . .' Fragment Number 29 sobbed, glancing at the professor nervously, 'because she has to believe in what she remembers, not what is happening before her eyes.'

'Well noticed,' the professor beamed her satisfaction. 'That's exactly why she is left alone. She holds her own beliefs, therefore nobody else believes her, not even her parents. As you have already seen from the previous footage, her mother failed to discipline herself in order to comply with the new regulations, so only she expressed negative responses. Such reactions in a public ceremony are obviously unacceptable.'

'It's not her fault,' Fragment Number 29 shook her head. 'It's not in her control. All she can do is wait for someone to come, to appreciate and share her memories. Otherwise she will never be able to accept her own thoughts.'

The professor smiled with curiosity. 'Why do you feel so strongly for her, Fragment Number 29? Don't you think she's pathetic? More precisely, pathologic? Nobody wants to protect her, because of her morbid inflexibility. You should be extremely proud of yourself, compared to her

150

conditions.' She whispered, her fingers slid over Fragment Number 29's hair. 'We will never leave you alone.'

'Ring around the roses, a pocketful of posies,' Fragment Number 29 responded with less anxiety, 'there are red roses around her, so she could convince herself . . .'

'No, there is nothing. When her parents come back from the meeting, all of them will realise that escapism is futile. Remember, what you have seen on the screen is merely a recollection from the past. The fidelity of the past can never be challenged, because The Great Calibration has already triumphed. Remembrance is not reconstruction, Fragment Number 29.'

The Great Calibration. If she could remember anything, would she remember the forthcoming events, the unforeseeable tomorrow? Fragment Number 29 gave the professor a perplexed look, without letting go of the little girl's roses.

Fragment Nineteen

Everything had to be done in a steady and invariable fashion. If a sequence of events had been triggered, everything else would continue to happen in the same way. The announcement of the One Country Principle was merely a milestone in the progress of the establishment of Monochromian ideology, which would soon be determined and implanted by The Great Calibration. There was no exception, not even the possibility for it. The black sky had prevented any opposition from emerging, because there was nothing to compare with.

The new year began, together with further reinforcement of the Principle. During the first two months, Irene and Mitchell had removed all the coloured decorations in their house, and had replaced the flowery wallpapers with plain white plastic films. The lilac curtains were gone, their original place taken by two layers of white blinds. Now they had almost nothing else to decolourise. Only the flowers in their garden could act as a reminder of the deceased colours, but most of them had withered because of light deficiency. It was early morning; the red spikes hanging down from the fence looked particularly disturbing under the black sunlight, infected by a lethargic brown hue. Irene sat in the living room on her own, next to the window. She glanced at the garden through the blinds, her eyes fixed at the yellow lining of her Siberian irises. When will they go? When will the last gleam of colour disappear? She thought, carefully wiping away the watery mist underneath. Her right index finger left some random lines on the window pane, as if she was attempting to produce a silhouette for the wilting creatures outside. A silhouette not restricted to the shape of the shadow itself, but to her own recollections.

Irene looked up to the sky. It would normally snow in February, but she could not tell the weather. When it snowed last year, everything was covered in white. Why did everything look so naturally beautiful then, even thought their colours could not be seen? The sky was sullen and grey, and there was almost no daylight; how could that be any different from this new substitute? She remembered seeing the same scenery somewhere else, a place where she had always enjoyed the cold winter. Why is everything so different now? Where is . . .

Her thoughts were interrupted by the noise of approaching footsteps behind her. Maybe this is the last chance to do it, before everything is too late. She took a deep breath, and turned back. She saw Felicity smile at her, leaning against her desk. Pink ribbons drooped from her plaits, in contrast with her dark purple dress. 'Where's daddy?' she asked, 'I thought we'd read the story together.'

'Quiet, Felicity, daddy is still in bed,' said Irene, putting a finger to her lips. 'Have you had enough sleep, my little Felicity? You don't have to get up this early.'

'I heard mummy going somewhere, so I just followed.' Felicity grasped Irene's arm. 'I thought it's still in the evening, because everything is so dark outside.'

Irene sighed, and stood up reluctantly. 'Felicity,' she fondled her hair, 'take off these ribbons, and change into your white pyjamas.'

'No, mummy, I don't want to take them off. I like pink and purple. You like blue, don't you, mummy? Why do you not wear it any more? Why do we all have to wear white?' Felicity shook her head, protecting the ribbons with the other hand. She was almost dragged along to the desk, when her mother tried to take out a folder from the bottom drawer.

'Listen to me, Felicity. How many times have I told you, that we can only have black and white?' Irene glared at her. 'Please, Felicity, be a good girl. Mummy and Daddy don't want you to get hurt, or anything. You will get used to all these, believe me. Everything will be fine.'

'But it didn't *used to* be like this! I wonder where all the colours have gone, I want to know why the sky has turned black,' cried Felicity. 'Mummy, I miss my hairpins and ribbons, I miss my flowers! You have taught me about all these flowers and colours, and I remember every single word from you!'

Irene held her in her arms; her voice began to tremble as she spoke again. 'Felicity,' she opened the folder with cautious determination, 'mummy wants you to be happy but you must understand, our happiness is defined by the circumstances that affect us every day. Before you were born, I had once imagined that this country would eventually change, that's why daddy and I decided to come back. Neither of us had ever expected that it was heading the other way, but we thought that at least we could teach you something valuable at home. So we did not send you to the Collective Nurturing Facility, and we read our stories to you.' She kissed Felicity, lost her balance and crumpled to her knees.

Felicity felt something watery on her face. 'Mummy, what happened, mummy?' she sobbed in panic, picking up the folder from the floor, 'I'm sorry, mummy, have I done anything wrong?'

'Don't worry, Felicity I'm just a bit tired. Do you want to hear the ending of mummy's new book?'

Irene panted, faking a smile with difficulty, 'It's the last page in this folder, let mummy read it for you.'

'It must have a happy ending,' said Felicity, sobbing, 'did the Flower Princess marry her Prince? Did she finally come back to his Palace?'

'Yes, of course they will live happily ever after, in a country full of colours and flowers. They will be as free as the birds in the blue sky.' Irene kissed her once again, before she turned to the last page. Forgive me, Mitchell, she thought, forgive me for letting our daughter remember. She doesn't want to forget, even if we have to. 'The Flower Princess and the Prince have made their garden even more beautiful than before,' continued Irene, 'amaryllis, lilac, lily-of-the-valley and forget-me-not. Red, purple, white and blue. The Flower Princess loves forget-me-not. It is the sacred pledge between her and the Prince. He is listening to the voice of their unborn daughter inside her body, but everything is so quiet. So, he thinks that the baby must be sleeping. The Princess looks a bit confused, because she still has not yet decided her daughter's name.' she turned to Felicity, 'Can you help the Princess, my little Felicity?'

Felicity blushed. 'Their daughter should have the most beautiful name,' she said, 'and . . . when she grows up . . . she will be the most beautiful girl in the world.'

'Yes, the Princess and her Prince agree with

you, Felicity. In fact, they have thought of you, before they fly back to the Palace, the Princess has always wanted to have a daughter like you. She insists that her daughter should be happier than herself, so she . . . she . . .'

Irene suddenly burst into tears. She embraced Felicity with all her strength, as if she was trying to stop a feather from being blown away in the storm. 'Felicity, my little Felicity,' she wailed breathlessly, 'remember us, remember mummy and daddy, remember our garden, our flowers. Promise me that you will look after yourself, safely and happily, please, my Felicity!'

Felicity did not weep. Instead, she kissed her mother with great affection and gratitude, as if she had already realised something. 'This is not part of the story,' she whispered softly, 'the Princess and her Prince will live happily ever after. Then the new Princess will remember. I promise you, mummy, I will remember. Wherever I am, even if I have to get rid of my ribbons, I will remember. Because I believe, and I know there must be another . . .'

'Irene! What are you doing here, Irene? Don't you they'll be coming soon?'

The door behind them squeaked open, and Mitchell dashed out from the bedroom. He stared at Irene, and snatched the folder from her. 'Are you insane?' he shouted, 'they could be watching us right now!'

'They? Who is "they"?' Felicity murmured, without looking at either of her parents. She seemed to be unaffected by her father's reaction.

They heard somebody knocking on the door; it sounded as if it was nothing violent, not even urgent. Yet they knew that they did not have the option to ignore it. Mitchell's face turned pale. 'Irene,' he shivered, 'they have arrived.'

'So we shall greet our guests,' Irene replied in a much calmer manner, although she could not hide her swollen eyelids.

Mitchell shoved the folder underneath the desk, and checked every drawer before he walked to the porch. He could clearly feel the pounding of his heart. It was not an unexpected response, even if he had been waiting for these visitors. A salty, metallic smell clung to his palm when he turned the door handle.

He saw a middle-aged woman in a black suit; she stood quietly by the doorstep, with an elegant and amiable smile on her pallid face. 'Is she ready to come with us?' she asked, staring at Mitchell, 'we very much appreciate your decision to hand her over to us. Education is something more important than you think, especially when you consider the fact that she has already missed the best time for it.'

'I think my daughter is ready,' answered Mitchell, nervously glancing at Irene and Felicity. He was not sure if she would say something contradictory to the woman, but he was piously hoping that she wouldn't.

The woman nodded her approval. 'Good,' she strode into the house, approaching Felicity. 'My colleagues and I from the Local Collective Nurturing Facility will take care of her. Your daughter . . . what's her number? You have never told us . . .'

Irene sprang up to hold her daughter, yet toppled backwards onto the floor. 'No, Mitchell, don't let her in! She is not on her own . . .' she cried, 'there are other people outside our house!'

The woman clenched Felicity's hand, and gave Irene a contemptuous glare. 'Why did you say that? I shouldn't be on my own anyway. Weren't you expecting "they", not "she", to pick up your daughter?'

'Mummy! I don't want to go anywhere, mummy!' Felicity screamed, unable to escape from the woman's commanding grasp. She looked at the woman imploringly, as tears began to accumulate in her eyes. 'Please, I don't want to leave my mummy and daddy. Where are you taking me? I don't know you!'

'Your parents would not help you, my uneducated little number,' the woman laughed with intimidating compassion, 'they *have chosen* to send you away from them. They want us to take care of you. Therefore, you will be officially admitted to our Collective Nurturing Facility from today.'

Felicity gasped; the woman stopped and stared

at her with interest, as if she was doing some kind of observation. 'No, this can't be true!' Felicity cried, yet she received nothing but silence. Mitchell turned his face away, and Irene lowered her head without saying a single word. Cold, suffocating silence paralysed her nerves, purging her last hope of protection.

'Separation anxiety is a useful thing,' said the woman, making a simple gesture towards the doorway. 'Are you ready to go as well?' she smiled again at Irene and Mitchell, 'perhaps your daughter will feel better, if you would like to cooperate with us one step further.'

Two men in black uniforms appeared behind her, like the shadowy phantoms from a delirious dream. One of them strutted towards Irene, swinging his electric baton before her eyes. 'You are a clever woman,' he sneered, 'but the clearest eyesight only belongs to the majority of people. Sweeping your unspeakable secrets under the carpet is no good; indoctrinating your daughter will not help you to spread your subversive thoughts. Because she is the hopeful, you are not.'

The woman untied the ribbons from Felicity's hair, and threw them at the other man. The man stepped back with disgust. 'My incorrect number,' she whispered, 'our facility is like a big family. I'm sure you will love it there. You have been contaminated by your parents, especially your mother, for too long. But it's not your fault. Your parents must be punished for their crimes.'

160

Crimes? My parents are criminals? Felicity shuddered, terrified by her own thoughts. Everything had been too sudden to be credible, too inexplicable for her to bear. She screeched in a paroxysm of fear, sadness and confusion, struggling to dissociate herself from the control of the woman's hands. Think about the Flower Princess, and her Prince. Think about their unborn daughter. She said to herself secretly, again and again, until an electric current pierced the air and smothered her voice.

Fragment Twenty

The professor had eventually switched off the screen. The shimmering lights in Room Ai darkened, and the indistinct humming noise in the background vanished into a solid form of cold quietness. Fragment Number 29 gazed at the ceiling listlessly as the colours faded away; the little girl's voice echoed in her mind, her image gradually dissolving into the invisible black hole created by her own eyes.

'What can you remember now, Fragment Number 29, having seen the film of that nameless girl?' asked the professor. 'It should have been very helpful. The correction of false remembrance is nothing dissimilar from the destruction of the mistake itself, especially when the memory is not unique.'

Fragment Number 29 slowly turned her head towards the professor, reaching for the support of her hands. 'That girl is not nameless,' she murmured, 'I remember, her name is Felicity. What happened to her parents in the end?'

162

'Answer my question, Fragment Number 29.' The professor grasped her trembling wrist. 'It does not matter any more. She is nothing but a number, a degenerate number. You must have remembered something.'

'Professor, I . . . I don't know. I felt as if I could empathise with that girl, as if I had gone through everything with her,' said Fragment Number 29. 'I know she cannot have been a part of my own memories, but . . . somehow our minds were connected together.'

'Why? Of course, you could have remembered her. You could have met her somewhere before, despite the fact that she is much younger than you.' The professor smiled, caressing the back of Fragment Number 29's hand with her white fingers.

Fragment Number 29 moaned when she touched the black scars on her forearm. 'No, professor, I can't have. This is only the second year of The Great Calibration, but she will not be calibrated until . . .' She suddenly stopped. A choking sensation of subliminal familiarity filled up her throat, as her own words desensitised the receptors under her cerebral cortex. She gave the professor a helpless glance.

The professor raised her eyebrow. 'What you have experienced here is what the little girl will experience. But she's different. She loved the Collective Nurturing Facility, not like you. She was the hopeful one.'

'She *was?*' Fragment Number 29 cried feebly. 'I'm confused. If both of us *had* gone through the same process, how could *we* have remembered different things?'

'We? Who is "we?"' The professor laughed. 'If there is *we*, I can tell you that you have always disappointed *us*, Fragment Number 29. Ever since your first day at the facility, you have always been a pain for your tutor, and for everybody else. How can you compare yourself with that girl?'

Fragment Number 29 flinched, and lowered her head. The little girl is the hopeful one, I'm not. The word *we* is not only inclusive, but also collective. The most important thing is that you must be aware of the *singularity* of this collective we. 'I do remember,' she said, 'my first day at the Collective Nurturing Facility.'

Her past had always appeared to be something strange to her. When she tried to recall the events that happened before she became a Fragment, it would always be like reading someone else's story in third-person narrative, rather than writing it herself. Perhaps it was because of the perpetual stillness in the classroom, she thought. In the everlasting trance-like state of mind, in the interminable labyrinth of isolation, she had successfully managed to alienate herself from her classmates. They could not disrupt her stream of thoughts, because they could not speak. Sitting in the last row, her 'older age' and 'ill-mannered behaviour' had become both her deterrent and stigma. She remembered being forced to wear the white uniform, when she struggled to keep her own pink-laced skirt. She hated the name badge in particular, because it was the same as everybody else's.

'Number 29 is not my name!' she shouted in front of the whole class, 'I'm not wearing this!'

Her classmates stared at her with blank expressions. They all seemed to be so comfortable, so self-content in their cotton blouses and skirts. None of them had any doubt as to why they were there, or what they were doing there. They were the products from the same batch of orders; their unanimous complexions scared her, yet she also felt pitiful for their emptiness. 'We shouldn't be wearing this.' She stressed her point by tearing off the badge from her blouse, and held it up towards her classmates. 'Can't you remember? We are not numbers! We once had our own names . . .'

'Shut up, you little polychromist,' her tutor yelled, with black flames of resentment flickering in her eyes. 'You are too dirty to become one of us. Don't even try to contaminate our children with your infectious propaganda. You are already nine years old, Number 29. None of us wanted to accept you to our facility! You are here because The Great Calibration is still in its early stages, and we have to do our duties in order to prepare for its forthcoming success! Otherwise we would stitch up your mouth and lock you up in the basement or somewhere safer.'

Number 29 moved back as her tutor hunched forward; a thread of delayed vigilance crept into her mind. 'You cannot change what I think,' she argued in a less passionate tone. 'I don't believe what you say. Even if you seal up the sky with black sheets and paint the whole world with white ink, there are colours somewhere. I remember seeing them!'

The tutor clutched Number 29's arms, and pushed her to the corner of the classroom. 'Nonsense!' she screeched, pressing down Number 29's shoulders with all her strength. 'You will pay the price for your incorrect ideology. There are only black and white in the entire world. Our bodies are made of black hair, black eyes, black blood and white skin, so is everything else.' She pointed backwards at the white puppet dolls with her thumb. 'If you don't self-criticise your thoughts and listen to us, you will remain a scandalous number forever, whereas all our young and hopeful monochromists will become the new generation of the Victorious Fragments!'

'I don't believe you! How can my own memories ever be wrong? How can you judge my thoughts by black-and-white measurements? How can you erase the past?' Number 29 battled to maintain the fluency of her speech, while finding it more and more difficult to stand steadily on her feet.

'We do not erase the past. It's you who has fudged up all those inaccurate memories, with your nefarious conspiracies to vitiate our collective interests!' The tutor snorted with a sinister grin. 'You said you've once had a name, and have seen a different colour. If you really do remember, tell us what they are! You said your blood is not black, prove it to us!'

'My name *is* . . .' Number 29 cried, but she was unable to finish the sentence. She could not remember. Her tutor nodded to her other pupils; their eyes brightened, as if they had come out of the continual vacuity by acting as the spectators of a failed rebellion. 'My name is . . .' Number 29 stammered, her voice being bleached away by her tutor's vindictive stare. She winced in anxiety. 'I don't remember. Why? I don't remember my own name!'

'You cannot tell us. Why should we believe you?' questioned her tutor. 'We've had enough of this nonsense. Put your badge back on and go to your seat! We shall punish you for your disobedience.'

'It's not disobedience, it is dissidence,' Number 29 wheezed, without discarding the sense of self-respect in her words. 'My blood is not black, not like you. I don't have to remember it . . . it is inside me.' She stretched out her arms, resisting the coercive force from her tutor. She released the needle in the back of her name badge, and placed it at her left wrist.

'I could clearly see the vessels under my skin. Now I just feel so lucky that I did not do it then.'

Fragment Number 29 looked at her chest, as if she had something missing there. Number 29 was another strange name for her. 'You wouldn't believe how I felt, if you had never experienced such feelings before.' She smiled at the professor, almost surprised at her calmness. 'When you watch yourself doing something incredibly outrageous, but you just couldn't help it.'

'I'm glad to hear that, Fragment Number 29. You are obviously getting better at understanding yourself,' replied the professor, 'but you had lied to me once. When we first met, and I asked you what colour your blood was and you said that you didn't know the colour. In fact, you were proud of it, weren't you? You *thought* you were different from everybody else, didn't you?'

'I feel very regretful, professor,' Fragment Number 29 sighed. 'Again, I just wanted to know the truth, the fact ... I still can't get rid of these memories, no matter whether they are fake or not. I envy the little girl in the film, because she enjoyed her days at the facility. As you know, my professor, I absolutely hated my tutor.'

'You'd rather stay at our Centre, since you feel privileged. At least you are free to use the word *I* here.' The professor held Fragment Number 29's wrist in her warm hands, as if she was to check her pulse. 'In return, you should have more trust in us. The truth, the fact is right in front of you, not only *inside* you. Why can't you believe us in the same way you believed the little girl? How is her story more convincing than anybody else's? Look at all these scars on your arm. Aren't they disgraceful? Do you remember who did them to you?'

Fragment Number 29 looked away. 'I don't know. But I would like to find out. There is so much confusion, so much pain in my brain . . . for some unknown reasons, I became so obsessed with one single idea that there is another country. I have been there myself, my dear professor. It's not my fault that I can't forget . . .'

'You can easily forget about everything if you want to,' said the professor. 'It won't be a long process, because I know the truth, I know the fact. You will become *we*, when you finally reach the point of total agreement with me.'

So, in order to discover the reality, I will have to forget everything? Fragment Number 29 asked herself in silence, and nervously peeked at her arm. She wondered if the little girl had the same scars.

Fragment Twenty-One

Somebody had mercilessly destroyed the purity of her white skin, and abandoned her in the abyss of infinite darkness. It was a form of negative reinforcement, although its effects did not seem to last very long. She had always believed that she was not on her own, until the moment she realised the benevolent indifference from those people around her. None of them wanted to listen to her, let alone speak with her. The impact of such despair and solitude was never to be forgotten, therefore she decided to maintain her memories for as long as she could, by keeping the wounds on her arm open and unhealed.

'My tutor locked me up in the basement for three weeks after that disruptive episode in the class. I thought they would never let me out again. The room was completely empty, without any kind of furniture, not even a bed. It had no windows, no light, nothing except a shabby blanket and a closed-circuit camera. It was so small that I could never lie down in a comfortable position. My tutor said it was a collective decision to punish me, and I believed her. For some reason, they did not allow me to wear that name badge any more. Maybe they had already deleted me from the register, and that would be the end of it.'

Fragment Number 29 had come back to her bed in Room Ai; the professor sat in a white chair next to her, holding her hand under the duvet. Nothing was connected to the metal bed frame, and the glass shards on the floor had been swept away. The screen was no longer there, as if it had never been there before. She wished that the professor could take off her gloves one day, so that she could feel the texture of her skin. It must be very soft and tender, she imagined. If the little girl from the film was here with her, would she fight for the professor's attention? A smile appeared on her fatigued face. 'Felicity's parents are novelists,' she whispered. 'I don't know how *her* tutor would treat her if she knew about her background.'

The professor put a finger to her lips. 'Her name is not Felicity, but you can use it if it helps. This is another privilege for you.' She patted Fragment Number 29's pillow, and rearranged her hair so she wouldn't have to see through her fringe. 'Novelists? This word sounds so distant for me. Nobody is allowed to write novels in Monochromia, Our Great Motherland. We do not need anything fictional.'

'We don't? But I remember seeing her mother

reading the book to her. The book about The Flower Princess and her Prince.'

'That was before The Great Calibration.' The professor smiled. 'One of the most important objectives of The Calibration is to thoroughly eliminate the production of instigative literature, including the possible attempts of doing so. This is especially exemplary in her parents' case. Her mother wrote about a fictional palace in a non-existing country.'

It was a non-existing country, but it had the appealing power to become real in her mind. Fragment Number 29 looked at her own reflections on the professor's silver-framed spectacles. She wanted to touch her ringlet, and her stiffly styled chignon. 'Will she remember the story, and tell it to her classmates at the facility? I can imagine her tutor's gloomy face.'

'Then you should continue to imagine, until the imagination becomes the truth. I don't personally know anything about her, her parents or her tutor; she wouldn't need somebody like me anyway,' said the professor. 'She can look after herself without pursuing autonomy or identity. She is happy to wear her name badge, become a number and eventually a Fragment.'

Fragment Number 29 tilted her head. 'Really? I would like to see the film footage for that . . . oh, sorry, she's only been staying at the facility for two years. If she had already become a fragment, she must have been the first one.'

The professor stared at her quietly, with a vague expression of unexpected solemnity. 'Fragment Number 29,' she said affectionately, 'do you think she will be happy, and proud of herself?'

'Probably she will be,' Fragment Number 29 replied, looking slightly surprised at the question. 'If she can easily forget everything.' She felt the professor's hand moving towards her neck; the silky surface of the white glove brought up a cooling sensation. She recognised a nostalgic emotion from the professor's voice, something reminiscent of her own interpretations of sorrow and mistrust. The little girl had promised her mother that she would never forget, so would she feel guilty if she did? Whatever she does, she is always guilty, or insane. Fragment Number 29 crossed her arms, and gripped the white glove with both of her hands. 'My professor,' she began to sob, as if it was an involuntary response, 'I feel sad when I think of Felicity. Her image overlaps with my own experiences at the facility, making it so difficult for me to imagine that she's happy to stay there.'

'It's natural,' the professor gave her a reassuring smile, 'because you have been mistreated by all those people. Locked up in a tiny cell without light, under constant surveillance from your tutor . . . there was barely any food for you, but none of this was the worst-case scenario for you.'

'I didn't do anything wrong . . . Number 29 didn't do anything to hurt anybody.' Fragment

173

Number 29 quivered. 'No, professor, I don't want to remember.'

'It happened on the last day of your confinement. Just think about how you felt when they opened the door, when you saw a path of light coming from the outside. Wasn't it a memorable experience? The moment you got out of the cell, the moment you could once again breathe in the air of freedom?' The professor lowered her voice; the soothing power of her smile sedated Fragment Number 29's nerves, slowly and gently, like a trickling stream of lavender essence oil. Lavender? Another unconscious association. She thought of its purple fragrance, but the flower itself remained colourless. Free imagination, this must have been the reason why they did *that* before they finally released her. Number 29 remembered something. Ring around the roses, a pocketful of . . . ring around the roses . . . She could never recall the last word of the rhyme, so she kept repeating the same line to herself. It must have annoyed her tutor, or whoever was responsible for watching her.

Number 29 began to draw on the grey wall with her fingers, outlining the petals of a rose. 'Ring around the roses, a pocketful of . . . ring around . . .' she mumbled. 'I don't remember, I don't remember . . . I've promised not to forget, but I can't remember, I can't remember . . .'

'What are you doing, Number 29? Stand still!' her tutor immediately howled at her though the microphone attached to the camera. 'You seem to

174

be enjoying your days here. If you continue to vandalise our facility, you'll be locked up here forever!'

'How does it make any difference? Vandalism, or anything – all the *crimes* I have committed – in the end it's all the same.' Number 29 looked up at the camera lens; the movement of her fingers slowed down, drawing a straight line across the middle of the rose's stem. She could not see the pattern herself, her hands slightly shaking in the cold, claustrophobic air in the cell. It was impossible for her to stand still. She could either squat down or lean diagonally between the opposite walls, but her legs were too weak to support her body, even though she had lost much weight due to malnutrition. The gleaming reflection on the lens appeared to be shining blindingly, like the vehement anger in her tutor's eyes.

Her tutor bellowed her dissatisfaction. 'We don't care if you'll stay here forever. Even if you kill yourself here, it's none of our responsibility. However, if your hopeless whims spread to other children in the facility, we'll take the most extreme measure to prevent it from happening. What have you been drawing on the wall? Imagine another child comes here and sees it – imagine her pure, peaceful mind becomes tarnished by your dirty brain!'

'I can't see anything here. My fingers have not left a single mark on the wall. It's my invisible picture, just like my thoughts.' Number 29 gazed at the wall. 'I still have the freedom of expressing my thoughts in a different way.'

'Your punishment is not for your crimes, but for your motives. If what you think is a gas, what you say will be a liquid. And what you write down is a solid. Do you understand this? Possibly you don't. Now, get your hand off the wall. Are you deaf? Get your dirty hand off the wall!' A grunting noise extruded itself from the microphone; Number 29 could visualise the muscles on her tutor's face twitching upwards. She glanced back at the camera. Instead of moving back, she inclined forward and scribbled down even more words and patterns.

'Number 29! Stop it now!' her tutor shrieked in rage, 'we will stop you!'

A spherical spark erupted from the seamless wall; its repulsing force spurned away Number 29's hand. She slumped into the opposite corner, yet her elbow received another dose of electrical discharge and was thrown into convulsions. Every movement of her body would result in an episode of shock, whenever her skin came into contact with the wall. The sparks had a glaringly blue colour, and seemed extraordinarily agitated when paralleled with a pitch-black background. Number 29 screamed in agony, as black blisters began to develop around her wrist and elbow. She panted and whimpered, too frightened to cry for help. Nobody would come to help her anyway. Nobody, there was absolutely nobody . . .

'How did you feel, Number 29?'

The door suddenly cracked open when she eventually collapsed. A beam of bright white light was directly projected at her face, but her pupils did not contract. Her tutor stood behind her, observing her listless eyes. Her uniform was dusty and frazzled, and there were holes with serrated edges in the sleeves. 'We are not expecting you to apologise,' said the tutor, 'because you're the hopeless, Number 29. Perhaps we should consider referring you to a more professional care system.'

Tears rolled down from Fragment Number 29's cheeks, wetting the professor's white fingertips. 'Nobody should go through anything like that,' she moaned, 'I wish they'd killed me then.'

'But you were released after that,' the professor said gently, almost pleased with her reactions. 'You could never find out exactly who pressed the button, or who sat behind the monitors. You should hold gratitude, not enmity, towards that person. Now, just imagine that somebody else did it to you. Imagine it happened somewhere else – for example, a non-existing country.'

Fragment Twenty-Two

Number 29's tutor placed a black document wallet on her desk, before her assistant came in and greeted her with a slip of paper. 'Our professor, the Victorious Fragment Number Nil, from the State Research Centre for Mental Refilling, is due to visit our facility in fifteen minutes.' She handed over the paper. 'Please sign your name here for the final confirmation.'

The tutor glanced at the paper with great satisfaction. 'We should have arranged the visit a long time ago.' She grabbed a pen from her drawer. 'So we could have disposed of that troublemaker.'

'Indeed, our facility has done everything to help Number 29, but there has been no improvement so far,' replied the assistant. 'At least it proves that the age of the child plays a pivotal role in her education process.'

The tutor nodded. 'However, her referral to the Centre must be kept a secret. Sending someone from our facility to another establishment damages our reputation . . . but it's really our last resort.'

'Perhaps she's the first minor to be sent there.'

'Yes, we can be sure she'll be very proud of herself for that!' the tutor said. 'The Centre is *not* a place for psychiatric care and treatment. It is a research laboratory! Number 29 is mentally ill, but we are not going to treat her by any means. Her illness is incurable.'

'But it's only the second year of The Great Calibration,' said the assistant. 'The process could take longer than we'd previously estimated.'

'She has to go through a different process! Whatever her age is, she will end up in the Re-education Committee with all the other deleted numbers, if she does not get refilled in the Centre. Our numbers can be calibrated in a variety of ways,' the tutor responded impatiently, tapping the front cover of the wallet. 'The children in our facility do not have to be refilled to become Fragments. The refilling process is basically designed for the hopelessly obstinate, the deviant polychromists.'

The word polychromist increased the assistant's nervousness. She slowly stepped back, and opened the door with cautious reluctance. 'We'd better be prepared for the visit. We're so glad that soon there will be no more pollution . . .' she stuttered before she left the office, 'from the evil polychromists.'

The tutor squinted at the clock on the wall. The

numbers under its glass case flashed constantly with white fluorescence, emitting a transient shadow into the air at every second. They disappeared and re-emerged, in a systematically calculated pattern. The interior of the office was covered in black wallpaper; unlike the classrooms, the offices at the Collective Nurturing Facility had their colours reversed. The black background enhanced the whiteness of the tutor's spotless overall, with the discordant decoration of her black scarf. She opened the first page of the wallet.

'Number 29, female. Born in 2031, at the Municipal Hospital of . . .' She whispered to herself, until a black blot on the paper stopped her reading. The name of the place was blocked out. Municipal? This term is no longer applicable. Capital, only the Capital exists.

She quickly skimmed over to the next line. 'Admitted to our facility in 2040, following the arrest of her former "parents". Continually engaged in negative reactionary speech and action; exhibited first signs of mental disturbance in the third month of admission. Tendency of self-injurious behaviours and self-destructive thoughts. Must be kept under strict guardianship. Diagnosis: unknown.'

The tutor blinked when a white shadow appeared behind the semi-transparent viewport in front of her. She stood up in a hurry, and turned the knob on the door. The womanly figure smiled at her. 'You must be the Victorious Fragment Number Nil from the Centre!' She held out her hand with an adulatory grin. 'Welcome to our Collective Nurturing Facility.'

'My colleagues call me "professor", not "Number Nil",' the Victorious Fragment returned quietly, and shook the tutor's hand without taking off her white gloves.

'Of course, our dear professor. Please sit down.' The tutor pulled out a black leather chair, pretending not to be astounded by the word *my*.

'Thank you.' The professor took her seat, staring at the tutor with a sense of occupational objectivity. Instead of a standard white overall, she was wearing a blouse and a long skirt, under the cloak of a crease-resistant white coat. Even her black scarf was arranged in a slightly different way. She tied back her hair in a tight chignon, so nothing else could darken her clear vision. 'So you are Number 29's tutor,' She crossed her arms. 'In your letter to me, you mentioned that you would like to refer Number 29 to our Centre? What is your reason for this decision?'

'For the sake of other children in our facility,' the tutor answered carefully. 'Number 29 is mentally ill. She's had a certain type of delusional disorder for nearly six months.'

'A delusional disorder? Can you give me some examples?'

'Oh, it's too shameful for us to repeat her noxious ideas, our dear professor,' the tutor winced, as if she would be punished for doing her duty. 'She claims that there is another country, a country full of colours, and . . . freedom.' Her lungs contracted spontaneously, and her pale face turned grey when she stammered out the last syllable. 'We utterly, utterly, oppose against this statement! It, it is absolutely pernicious to Our Great Motherland. The One Country Principle is indisputable, and the infallible dominance of Guardian M, Our Great Leader, is . . .'

The professor cleared her throat with a dispassionate expression. 'Perhaps you should directly report her to the Re-education Committee, not to our research Centre.' She shrugged. 'This could either be a disorder, or a crime. Does Number 29 genuinely believe in these statements?'

'Her excuse is that she didn't make up these dangerous thoughts, she *remembered* them. She was born *before* The Great Calibration, our dear professor,' the tutor explained anxiously. 'We know that she could not have remembered anything, because Monochromia, Our Great Motherland, has always been the same, and will continue to be the same.'

'Even before the Calibration?' the professor asked calmly. 'All delusions are formed upon a realistic basis. The key to solving the problem is to understand the difference between perception and *reception*. A natural occurrence can be perceived from many different perspectives, but there's only one way in which it will be received and stored. In other words, as soon as you remember something, the event itself becomes fixed by your own interpretation. Our Centre concentrates on the perception part of the process. Our ultimate aim is to totally eliminate the possibility of a second perspective, before it reaches the final stage.'

'Oh, the theories are too complex for us.' The tutor shook her head. 'We do apologise for our ignorance, but doesn't the term Refilling refer to the renewal of pre-stored memories?'

The professor did not reply immediately. She flipped through the black wallet, and stopped at a bookmarked page. The phrase *self-injurious* attracted her attention. She lowered her voice, glancing at the tutor with a tentative smile. 'Yes, it does. But it also involves deliberate exposure to certain external stimuli that will induce even more delusions and hallucinations to the subject, which could sometimes result in a series of highly undesirable side-effects,' she explained. 'If Number 29's alleged remembrance of "the other country" is made fictional for a purpose, then she will be convicted of subverting state stability; if not . . .'

'We are very sorry to interrupt, our dear professor,' the tutor cried, 'but her so-called "remembrance" must be false, with or without a purpose!'

'So why do you need me from the Centre? If Number 29 is plotting some kind of conspiracy, the Re-education Committee will take care of her. We can consider the option of refilling, if the re-education process does not work. However, what is *your* purpose? Do you want to simply get rid of her, or help her to regain her sanity?' the professor held up the wallet. 'In fact, I have something to ask you. What is Number 29's "self-injurious behaviour", and why did she do it?'

'She attempted to slit her wrist with the needle on her name badge, because . . .' Once again, the tutor stumbled over her words. 'She wanted to show us that her blood had a different colour . . . not black . . . oh, please don't worry, our dear professor, we successfully stopped her!'

'Maybe you shouldn't have. I'd like to see her do it again.' The professor sat back in a relaxed posture. 'To be perfectly truthful with you, I think it's highly likely that her remembrance *is* true. In that case, our Centre will need her memories. Number 29 is not an attention-seeker; it is the irreconcilable conflict between the perception and the received information that triggers her disorder.'

The tutor gaped at the professor in disbelief. 'It is actually a psychiatric disorder? So the Centre is going to deal with it?'

'Isn't this what you are expecting to hear from me? However, it's still too early for our Centre to take the responsibility. She might need to be refilled, but we have to determine the nature of her illness. Is it persecutory delusional disorder, paranoid psychosis, post-traumatic stress disorder, or something completely unknown?'

The professor took the wallet, and slowly stood up. You are ignorant indeed, she thought. Only *my* Centre will succeed in transforming Number 29. 'Please do not assume that mental refilling is merely a procedure to be undertaken as a routine. Our Centre will need subjects like Number 29 to perfect the system. Before we officially diagnose her symptoms, we shall wait for another event to happen.' She looked at the tutor proudly. 'Number 29's parents will participate in their first re-education lecture next month. Please make sure that she attends as well, because I will be there. I will decide what she needs from you, or from our Centre.'

'Her parents ... you have heard about her parents, our dear professor? Yes, they are the first couple of numbers to be re-educated, calibrated and deleted. Is the Centre involved in this, too?'

'You are obviously very passionate about making enquiries,' said the professor. 'Strictly speaking, our Centre is not an executive unit for the Calibration. We are a scientific establishment. Our mission is to accelerate the calibrating process when necessary, using our expertise on operant conditioning, coercive persuasion and other relevant psychiatric methodologies. I shall take her documents for assessment.'

The fluorescent clock on the black wall was still flashing, although the tutor was unable to recall the original numbers. The professor returned the chair to its previous position, saluted with three of her white fingers and left the office. She disliked the idea of saying 'goodbye', especially when the conversation was considered unproductive. The wallet was not essential to her research, but she had developed a *personal* interest in Number 29's case. Whatever it is, a crime or a disorder, it will be my honour to solve the problem. Faulty perception causes incorrect reception, yet it's never too late to reverse the effects. The cause is the consequence, and vice versa. Those Collective Nurturing Facilities should never overestimate their importance; they do nothing except providing a good range of samples for our Centre. Remembrance, remembrance is futile. Everything will lead to the final calibration of your psyche, no matter what kind of process is the most suitable for you.

She laughed secretly, imagining how Number 29 would have proven that her blood was not black. She looked forward to seeing Number 29 in person.

Fragment Twenty-Three

'If I could ever have predicted that you would become such a precious sample, I'd have brought you to the Centre when I first read your records. However, Fragment Number 29, you are more than a subject for me.'

The professor rolled up Fragment Number 29's left sleeve, gazing at the black scars from her physiotherapy. She caressed her wrist, as if her white gloves could displace the wounds with purity and tenderness. Fragment Number 29 slowly moved her head towards the professor, her line of vision wandering into the air. 'Professor,' she whispered sobbingly, 'I didn't mean to hurt myself. Someone else did it.'

'I'm not suggesting that you did. Your suffering comes from a different country, as you have remembered it yourself.' The professor smiled. 'I trust you. You did not make it up for a sinister purpose, your remembrance is real. It must have been so painful for you, when nobody at the facility believed you. But I'm different, Fragment Number 29. I believe you.'

Fragment Number 29 could not control the wrenching feeling inside her chest, as if it would contort her heart and explode at any time. The meaning of trust was dissolved and saturated in her tears, although she was unable to explain it in words. Professor, professor, who are you? She asked in silence, staring at the professor with devotion and gratitude. Are you my . . . ? Her lips trembled, yet she was too nervous to utter a single word.

'Even if your tutor thought that our Centre is not a psychiatric hospital, or any kind of place for treatment, we wanted to help you. We need your memories, you must understand. Do you remember this? Happiness is nation-specific,' the professor continued with forceful gentleness, 'you have been abducted to another country . . . by a strange man. He has inflicted pain and sorrow on your vulnerable heart, by promising that he will love you. Then he sends you back here, because you're no longer useful to him. He knows that nobody here will believe your memories.'

The light tubes on the ceiling began to fluctuate, when Fragment Number 29 slowly narrowed her eyes. White lines interlocked with one another, like the restless waves across an opaque pond. Another country? Where is it? The letter *I* formed a watery shadow in her mind, but it was soon dispersed into another path of light. 'I can't remember,' she cried in panic. 'Why? Where is it? I can't remember . . .'

'You can't remember, because that country does not exist. It's something in your mind, but it's also real. Your illness is caused by the deviation from the factual reality,' the professor explained, carefully taking out a small metal box from underneath Fragment Number 29's bed.

Fragment Number 29 tried to sit up when the professor's hand left her, but she made no real movement. 'What is the difference, my professor?' she asked helplessly. 'The perceived reality and the received memories . . . are they not in accordance with each other? I want to find out the truth . . . I want to go back to that country.'

'Because he promised you? You don't even know the name of that country,' said the professor. 'You can't go there on your own, it's too dangerous. I need to go with you, so I can protect you from that man.'

'No, he won't hurt me. But you're welcome to come, my professor . . . you'll love that place. I do, I do know the name, I just can't remember.' A gleam of hope came into Fragment Number 29's eyes; she gave the metal box a nervous glimpse, as if it contained all her inaccessible memories.

The professor lifted up the box, and placed it on her lap. 'I will not interfere with anything you do there, unless it's something of national interest. We are at war with the other country, remember. We're going to confront our enemies *again.*' She removed the lid, 'Hopefully you'll be convinced of the fact this time.'

'What is it? What's in the box?' Fragment Number 29 inclined towards the professor with difficulty. 'I don't want any more tablets.'

'So we use intravenous injection.' The professor picked up an automatic injector, smiling at Fragment Number 29 with soothing confidence. She pushed away the duvet, and removed the sterile membrane from the tip of the injector. The syringe itself was made of non-transparent polythene, so nobody could tell whether it contained a liquid, or something else. Perhaps it was empty. Fragment Number 29 thought, it could be a placebo.

'Is this part of my refilling process?' she asked, watching the syringe approaching her left arm. 'When will it complete? I'm scared, my professor. Every time when I wake up from my dreams, I feel detached from the real world.'

The hidden needle entered Fragment Number 29's body with a sharp click, and a cold solution flowed into her bloodstream. She did not feel any discomfort; it instantly tranquilised her mood, like the warm touch from a beloved stranger. 'You are not going to dream, my dear compatriot. What you will see is not an illusion, because I will be there with you,' said the professor. 'Your journey will not last very long. The final destination is always here, in Monochromia, Our Great Motherland. You will eventually realise how much we have done for you.'

'If I know the truth, will it make me any happier? When the received information re-adjusts itself and harmonises with the perceived imagery, will it bring me less uncertainty?' Fragment Number 29 murmured, before her voice vanished into silence. My professor is watching me, I can feel her holding my hand. My professor says that she trust me, so I must not disappoint her again, she said to herself sorrowfully, in the assumption that she would arrive at a different country. The white air in Room Ai did not disappear when she closed her eyes; instead, a soft plume of colourful fragrance invaded all her senses.

Colours. Fragment Number 29 blinked, unable to recognise their origin. Colours, thousands of colours were dancing in the form of iridescent spheres, as if they were falling down from the broken facets of an opal. She could taste the refreshing sweetness of chamomile in the air, and the smell of freshly baked cakes with yellow and blue icing. She heard the laughter of a young girl. Felicity. She held out her hand, fumbling about in the pallid darkness surrounding her. My little Felicity.

Her voice amalgamated with that of another woman. She welcomed her with an invisible embrace, and everything else began to materialise. The first thing she saw was the woman's sweet smile, and her ringlet-framed face. She was wearing a blue velvet gown, with an aquamarine pendant on her neck. Fragment Number 29 crossed her arms instinctively, looking at the woman in timid admiration. 'My little Felicity.' The woman gave her a loving stare. 'Do you know how much we missed you?'

'We? My name is not Felicity...' Fragment Number 29 was intrigued by her sweet voice; she was standing in front of her, so close to her that the silky texture of her dress seemed stiff and unreal. Her field of vision was almost restricted to the woman only, although the petals at her feet revealed the fact that she was in someone's garden.

'Yes, you are my Felicity.' The woman fondled her hair. 'Daddy and I have made some fruitcakes for you. Which colour of icing do you prefer?'

'No, I'm sorry, I'm not Felicity. My name is Flora Iris.'

The woman's smile froze for a moment, before she started laughing. 'Stop joking with mummy. Flora Iris is mummy's name, and your name is Felicity, Felicity Iris.'

'I'm afraid you got the wrong person, Felicity is...' Fragment Number 29 said, pointing at somewhere behind the woman. The full picture began to emerge as her fingers moved around, as if she was applying strokes of different colours to a blank canvas board. A man and a little girl were sitting in the far end of the garden; white vapours escaped from the porcelain teapot on the table next to them. The girl's appearance was inconsistent with her own impression of Felicity Iris. Her skin had a pinkish tone, and her hair was not black. The colour was called hazel. The purple ribbons on her lilac dress glimmered, as if they were beckoning Fragment Number 29 to come closer.

'Daddy, mummy's coming.' The little girl smiled at Fragment Number 29 as she walked towards her; her eyes were light green, with the slightest tint of grey shades. The man stood up to greet her, yet with less sincerity. He had even more brilliant colours than the girl, and the colour of his eyes was a much purer green. His blond hair shone under the sunshine, in contradiction with his impassive expression.

'My Flora? Welcome back to Iridescia.'

His greeting was possibly the simplest form that Fragment Number 29 had ever expected to hear, but it was powerful enough to strike her with flooding emotions. She was overwhelmed by a frantic impulse to hug that man, so tightly that their bodies would melt into each other. Iridescia, the unique name of the other country! Flora Iris, the incarnation of her deprived identity! Suddenly tears filled up her eyes to the brim, and she began to weep.

'Edwin,' she cried out the man's name, 'I'm here, I'm back to Iridescia! You have promised me . . .'

'But you have failed to remember me,' Edwin Iris replied coldly. 'You did not trust me.'

'I didn't choose to leave here!' Fragment Number 29 whimpered, 'I just wanted to bring another colour to Monochromia . . .'

'Stop arguing, daddy!' the little girl cried, gripping Edwin's arm. 'She didn't do anything wrong. She just wanted Felicity to be happy . . .'

Fragment Number 29 knelt down to hold the girl in her arms. She looked up to Edwin, as if he was no longer someone intimate to her. 'Felicity is crying, Edwin. Our daughter is crying . . .' She kissed the girl's forehead. 'Sorry, Felicity. Mummy and Daddy are not arguing.'

'What are you talking about? I don't have a daughter. Flora had just suffered a miscarriage, so please don't upset her again!' Edwin strode forward, and embraced the woman in the blue gown. 'My wife is depressed, because she was unable to return to Iridescia. But everything's fine now,' he whispered to the woman, 'everything she has is everything she has here.'

The woman glanced at Fragment Number 29 with some kind of confusion. 'Felicity? You are Felicity, aren't you? We've been waiting for you to come back . . .'

'No! Felicity is *my* daughter! She's here, Felicity is here with me!'

Fragment Number 29 screamed, and collapsed onto the frail body of the little girl. She was still smiling, without looking at anywhere. The warm radiance from her hair was defeated by the grey trails in her crystalline eyes, as if she had nothing more to share with the strange visitor to her garden.

Fragment Twenty-Four

Edwin Iris held the woman even closer; her black ringlet drooped over her right shoulder, caressing the semi-transparent buttons on his navy blue shirt. 'She will not harm you any more, my Flora,' he whispered fondly, looking into the distant scenery behind the colourless fence. 'You are different. You are special, unique. I do regret it, my Flora. I shouldn't have taken such an impulsive action when I first met that woman. Sympathy does not equal love or responsibility, my Flora. My vanity had made you suffer. I am so sorry, my Flora.'

'Felicity,' the woman sobbed, 'I want my daughter back.'

'I know, I know, but that woman there is not our daughter. She is an intruder.' Edwin glared at Fragment Number 29. 'She'll leave our house soon.'

Fragment Number 29 cried in despair, without letting go of Felicity's hand. 'No, Edwin, I cannot leave Iridescia. I love this country, because I love you, Edwin!'

The woman glanced at Fragment Number 29 with a mixture of self-contradictory emotions, scorn and compassion. She kissed Edwin, with fervent tears smouldering in her eyes. 'Like dissolves like,' she said. 'You are not Felicity, and you can't steal my name, my identity. You shouldn't be here.' She wiped her eyes; the affable smile had disappeared. She clutched Felicity's fragile shoulders, dragging her away from Fragment Number 29. Felicity fell onto the woman's bosom, as if it was somewhere she had always belonged.

'Felicity! You said she's not your daughter!'

Fragment Number 29 floundered through the indiscernible barriers around her; the soft petals on the floor seemed to have become rows of immovable pebbles, delicate but menacing.

'Felicity? Who is she? Nobody else is here.' The woman blinked, leaning against Edwin's lenient chest. Felicity stood in the middle, forming the perfect composition for a family photograph. Yes, a family photograph. If Edwin had a different complexion, it would be reminiscent of Fragment Number 29's own parents, if she could remember.

'Stop acting Fragment Number 29. Don't disappoint us again,' the woman said slowly. 'I'm Flora Iris now, Edwin Iris's wife. This is the fact, the truth. Are you satisfied?'

'You are from Monochromia?' Fragment Number 29 gasped in fear, before she lost her balance again. The sweet voice of a young woman was no longer there. 'Edwin, she is . . . please keep away

197

from her!' She uttered the words in involuntary despondency. 'She's the *insurgent* ... from Monochromia!'

'What does it matter, my dear compatriot? He loves me. His love for me is genuine, not like you.' The woman laughed proudly. 'Your true love is not for him – it is for an illusion, a virtual image of a non-existing country. Am I correct?'

'You promised that you wouldn't interfere!' Fragment Number 29 shouted at the woman. She could not move any closer, as if her body was trapped by the restraining tenderness of the petals. 'Of course I love Edwin,' she sobbed. 'You don't understand. You need nothing from him!'

The black scars on her arm were once again exposed, as she held out her hand towards Felicity. Felicity cringed at the sight of the scars, yet she did not express any fear on her bleak face. The woman covered Felicity's eyes. 'Don't let her touch you, my dear Felicity. She will contaminate you.' She stared at Fragment Number 29. 'Promise? I have never promised you anything, Fragment Number 29. I need nothing from him. What are you insinuating?'

No, this cannot be the truth. This is not Edwin, and this woman in blue ... is someone from *the Centre*. I should not have remembered anything from Monochromia, because Iridescia is the only country! Fragment Number 29 covered her face helplessly; she looked at Edwin in the last hope of retrieving the happy memories from his mind, but she received nothing. His eyes were totally fixed on the woman, as if she was the only person in his world. He could not recognise Felicity, or anybody else. 'What have you done to him?' she cried. 'You're not Iridescian. He cannot love you! What do you need from him?'

The woman shivered in a fanatic burst of laughter; she hid away her face behind Felicity's frail body, as if she was unable to suppress the flow of neurotransmitters in her brain. She panted, striving to take back her breath. 'Oh . . . sorry, I shouldn't laugh, but . . . how could you ever say things like that, Fragment Number 29? It makes my nerves itch. I must have done something nasty to him, isn't this your real thought? I am not Iridescian, what about you? I don't need to be Iridescian to be loved. You are too obsessed with your vanity, and it hurts both Edwin and I.'

Edwin Iris frowned. He fondled the woman's chignon with a deep sigh, avoiding any eye contact with Fragment Number 29.

'Look at me, Edwin. I have never denied that I love Iridescia, but it's different! Everybody in Iridescia loves their home country.' Fragment Number 29's arm drooped powerlessly, yet still suspending in the air. 'My love for you is true. I still remember everything, every moment that we shared together!'

'Don't even try to muddle up the *facts*, Fragment Number 29,' the woman said in her characteristically sombre tone. 'Iridescia is not your home country.'

It is a fact. It is the most unshakable and undisputed fact. Therefore, I want to prove that it does not have to remain a fact forever. The resonating voice inside Fragment Number 29's skull slowly spoke; her pupils dilated in relief. Yes, it does not have to be a fact. Even the most basic fact could be changed under certain circumstances. I belong here, and I deserve nothing else.

'You are a brilliant self-hypnotist,' the woman sneered. 'But it cannot assist you in evading the truth. The truth is far more sophisticated than a simple fact, *my dear compatriot.* Iridescia does not exist.' She dabbed at Felicity's cheeks with her velvet sleeve. 'Nor does this girl. When necessary, *we* will make Iridescia, or whatsoever, exist. But in your case, it doesn't work well because of this girl.'

'My compatriot. We . . .' Fragment Number 29 mumbled subconsciously. The familiarity of these phrases sharpened the woman's feminine figure, smudging and twisting it into a ruthless statue. Her camouflage evanesced, unveiling the long forgotten sense of trenchancy and scientific precision behind her silver-rimmed spectacles.

'No! Let go of my daughter!' Fragment Number 29 screeched in horror. 'Edwin! Please, trust me! This woman is not your Flora! She will . . . she will . . .' Darkness flashed through her mind. Edward Innes stood still in a mechanical posture, as if his limbs were controlled by a bundle of invisible strings. A sly smile clung up to the woman's nonchalant lips.

'So, who is Flora Iris?' The woman shrugged. 'Who is Felicity Iris? Neither of them exists as an entity. However, there is one advantage about being in Iridescia.'

'You said Iridescia is a non-existing country. How can you be here if Iridescia is not real?' Fragment Number 29 cried anxiously, incapable of re-activating her legs. She gasped. The fragrance in the air had paralysed her. It was not for inducing pain, or any temporary effect.

'Of course it's not temporary, Fragment Number 29! You are smart enough to realise this tiny change in your body. Everything I do is for a single purpose.' The woman paused and started braiding Felicity's hair. Felicity smiled at her affectionately.

Fragment Number 29's heart was boiling with hatred. I hate you. She glowered at the woman, I would love to stab you to death.

'Well, no hurry. You can stab me whenever and wherever you fancy. Oh . . . did I say *fancy*?' The woman cleared her throat and continued, 'Never mind. I am in Iridescia!' She squinted at Fragment Number 29. 'The advantage of being in Iridescia is that you are allowed to see what you cannot see in real life. Similarly, you can use all the meaningless words, like fancy. And all these psychedelic colours.'

'No, you cannot. These colours are not for you! You know nothing apart from black and white,' Fragment Number 29 argued with desperate courage. 'I don't know how you came here, but you don't belong here!'

'You invited me here, Fragment Number 29. I have never wanted any of these colours. I came here to help you. You want to find out the colour of your blood, don't you? I asked you the same question eleven years ago, and you have never provided a satisfactory answer.'

'It is dark red. It is the colour of my blood!'

'It has another name, a more beautiful name. Edwin knows it. Has he not told you yet? It's the colour of *Amaranthus caudatus*,' the woman whispered, gently rubbing her face against the nape of Felicity's neck. 'Ring around the roses, a pocket full of posies.' Her hand sidled along Felicity's back, and halted abruptly.

'The rhyme. How do you know the rhyme?' Fragment Number 29 trembled. Something will happen. She held her breath involuntarily while tracking down the movement of the woman's heavily gloved fingers. Something inevitable will happen. Once again, she looked up to Edwin Iris. There was no response from him. 'Tell me, what have you done to Edwin? You must have changed something! What happened to him?' she exclaimed; a gush of tears obscured her vision with a pricking sensation.

'We don't need him at this stage, do we? Just

wait for him to tell you the name of ... this colour.'

A cluster of *Amaranthus caudatus* came into full blossom before Fragment Number 29's eyes. The light lilac colour of Felicity Iris's dress faded away rapidly as the red spikes inundated her chest. The red, red spikes trickled down and solidified into a translucent bouquet; yet it was soon dissolved and absorbed by even more red spikes, pouring out from Fiona's throat without scruple. The spikes strangled her before she could scream for help, intensifying and accelerating the progression of her anguish. Fragments of the creamy spikes sprinkled onto the woman's professionally disciplined arms; hundreds of pungent petals flitted up and down at her feet. A man's voice landed on the tender tip of the longest spike, nimbly and tranquilly. The alternative name for dark red ... is crimson, my Flora. Remember? This was the last colour you saw. Crimson.

'It's good for her, Edwin. It is the best proof of her identity, because she could only exist in oblivion. Iridescia is the visualisation of oblivion.' The woman put down her scalpel and leaned against the wall. 'Oh, don't look at me like that, my compatriot. Are you wondering where I got my scalpel from? I would never be able to use it without your authorisation.' She grinned sweetly, sniffing at the aqueous petals on her palm. 'Don't worry, it is not the colour of her blood. How could I let my own daughter bleed? Her blood is not crimson, Fragment Number 29. It is black, purely black. Perhaps it would appear crimson in Iridescia, had it been a real country.'

Black. I would love to stain my blood black, so that I can test its validity itself. Iridescia, how can I love you more, Iridescia? You endowed me with everything precious in my life, but now you have destroyed them without mercy. Where are you, Edwin? Where are you, Felicity? The mesmerising fragrance of the flowers has never disappeared. Crimson. Thank you for teaching me another colour, Edward. I wish you had never betrayed me.

'Professor! We must go back, professor!'

Fragment Number 29 opened her eyes for a final glimpse of the garden. Everything was so vividly vague, so painfully pacifying. Go back? We are going back to nowhere. Iridescia is the only country. Is Iridescia the only country? There must be another country, *the other* country. It should be a highly enjoyable process. A gloomy noise came out from her lungs when she strived to speak; she saw her own brain break into splinters.

The woman in white coat turned back, standing in front of an enormous screen. It was the most innocent form of white that Fragment Number 29 had ever seen. Edwin Iris saluted, touching his forehead with three of his dedicated fingers. He was wearing a black uniform.

Fragment Twenty-Five

Perhaps it does not matter any more. The colour of one's blood . . . could be anything. Is transparency a colour? No, it is an optical property. Any colour could be transparent under certain circumstances. Including black and white? No, only black and white. But black cannot be transparent. Why? How about white? The transparent type of white is colourless. You cannot see it if it's colourless. Why? Look at the glass ceiling. It is transparent, yet you know it's there. Can you call it colourless?

'I can see the black sky . . . beyond the ceiling. It is not transparent . . . it is black.'

Fragment Number 29 murmured semi-consciously. She had been sent back to the Intensive Care Unit, lying on her stainless steel bed with her cosy duvet. The liquid crystal screen was somehow removed from her bedside and was displaced by a white box. She could not see what was attached to the box; it could be anything, such as a handle, a wheel, or a lever. Whatever it is, it will be of some kind of use. Nothing was dripping down from above. No black rubber tubes, no glass jars, no needles or tourniquets. Everything in the room was white. The professor was sitting in a white armchair beside the box; the whiteness of her coat had combined with the whiteness of the surroundings, as if she was fixated to the room itself as an indispensable component. If I could control my body, Fragment Number 29 thought, I would hold her hand and hug her.

'What happened, Fragment Number 29? Why are you crying?' asked the professor. 'Don't cry. Everything is fine, Fragment Number 29. What makes you feel so sad?'

'I have lost everything,' Fragment Number 29 sobbed. 'My beloved man and my daughter. Somebody murdered her. She was killed before my eyes!'

The professor stroked her fringe with a loving look. 'I am sorry to hear that. Can you remember who killed her, or where you were?'

Fragment Number 29 shook her head with difficulty; in fact, she was not even sure if she actually did shake her head. 'I don't remember. She was killed by an invisible force. I could not do anything to help her, I was confined in a room somewhere. All I saw was red, red spikes, and they were spreading everywhere.'

'We don't have red here, Fragment Number 29. Only black and white exist in Monochromia, Our Great Motherland. Where did you see that red colour?' The professor gently placed her right forefinger on Fragment Number 29's pale lips. A current of unspoken warmth flowed through her white glove.

The poignant fragrance of your body temperature is always with me, my dear professor. I don't have to remember anything painful. I don't want to remember anything anyway. Fragment Number 29 narrowed her eyes and smiled, without any actual feeling of her expression. 'It must be . . . somewhere else. I saw that colour . . . in a different country. There were many other colours as well, but I have forgotten their names.' Her smile gradually faded away. 'Why do I feel sad, professor? My chest hurts when I think about the other country.'

'Because it is the place where you were eternally deprived of everything you loved. The evidence is the red colour of your daughter's blood. If it happened in Monochromia, Our Great Motherland, the blood would have appeared black.' The professor softened her sweet voice and caressed Fragment Number 29's face. 'That country is our enemy, Fragment Number 29, my dearest *compatriot*. It is a country of pain and sorrow, as you have already experienced . . . it killed your parents and your daughter. So, what shall we do? We must have revenge. We must annihilate that country, in order to sustain and protect our interests. You should be very proud of the fact that you are playing a vital role in our mission.'

'Am I really? What have I done?' Fragment Number 29 panted faintly, 'I can't even remember the name of that country.'

'But you have successfully arrested its leader,' the professor explained. 'Now he is under our control and surveillance. You ought to be very pleased, Fragment Number 29. He is the man who has invaded your mind and betrayed you. All your suffering began when he abducted you to *Iridescia*, the non-existing country.'

Iridescia, the non-existing entity. It is called Iridescia. I have promised that I will never forget its name. Who is its leader? Where is this country? He did not *abduct* me, I was waiting for him to go there with me. Although he has betrayed me and left me bleeding in darkness, Iridescia itself is . . . it is . . . Millions of polychromic petals rained down from the black sky like silent tears. Fragment Number 29 heard a cacophonic shriek when they landed on her bed, streaking the air with a series of white trails. 'It is an important place,' she mumbled, 'whatever it has done to me it is an important place.'

'Of course it is, Fragment Number 29. Iridescia is of great *negative* importance. It is the negative region of an everlasting number line, the mirror image of a chiral molecule. We can only permit one of them to exist, which is the positive region. The opposition of monochromism is polychromism; similarly, the opposition of Monochromia, Our Great Motherland, is Iridescia.' The professor grinned. 'Any deviation from the positive region will evoke instability, turmoil and therefore, misery of our glorious citizens.'

'It has not caused anybody else to suffer. I am the only victim,' Fragment Number 29 cried in fatigue. 'This pain here in my chest is killing me. I feel as if my lungs are being filled up with molten iron, when you say the word Iridescia . . . and that man . . . Edwin Iris . . . when you were standing together, I felt as if . . .' She groaned in a twinge of suppressed heartbeat. 'My professor . . . are you . . .'

'I remember hearing you say the same phrase so many times,' said the professor, 'What is it? Don't be afraid of telling me. Everybody has left you now, but my love – *our* love – is unconditioned.'

Fragment Number 29 took a deep breath. Somehow she felt it was the only opportunity for her to say it, although it was already beyond her control to make a decision. 'You have always, always reminded me of my mother. This idea brings so much pain to me, but, my dear professor . . .' She paused; her voice trembled in intense expectation. 'My dear professor . . .' she continued after receiving an approving look from the professor, 'are you . . . my mother?'

The professor smiled. 'Does this suggest that Edwin Iris is *your* father?'

'No, I remember that both of my parents were killed during the Calibration . . . no, it can't be true. The Calibration only started two years ago . . .' Fragment Number 29 muttered, almost losing the coherence of her speech. 'Edwin . . . Felicity . . . no, my professor, I don't know. Am I Felicity's mother? Are you . . . my mother?'

'Two years ago? I'm surprised that you're still confused, Fragment Number 29. Which year do you think we are in?' The professor inclined her head with some kind of professional interest. 'Probably that's why you ask such illogical questions. We are in November 2052, two years *after* the total success of The Great Calibration.'

Anxiety submerged Fragment Number 29's nerves. 'November 2052?' she cried, almost pleased with the unforeseen fact. 'No wonder I have met Edwin and Felicity before. I have been in Iridescia since . . .'

'Shall I say it again? Edwin and Felicity Iris do not exist anywhere. They are purely imaginary. However, your syndrome is an entirely normal phenomenon, my compatriot. That's why we are looking after you in the Centre's Intensive Care Unit.' The professor whispered, 'Your suffering will end soon, I promise. You will feel no more pain or sorrow, when the refilling process completes. We are nearly there, Fragment Number 29. Physiotherapy has proved an ineffectual treatment to you, so we will try something else. I am sure you will feel much better this time . . . with our chemotherapy.'

Fragment Number 29 squinted at the black sky

under the cloak of the colourless ceiling. Its unfathomable darkness glittered in her dangerously harmless eyes. 'Then who is my mother? Who are Edwin and Felicity? Will I be able meet them up again after this treatment?'

'Definitely. Everything will come back to normal, and you can do whatever you like with your own body.' The professor patted her oblivious hand. 'You will be happy and free.'

'Why are you doing all these things for me, professor, if you are not my mother?' Fragment Number 29 whimpered feebly. 'You don't have to save me or do anything. I am the malfunctioning cell, the anomaly.'

Intermittent words and phrases jerked out of her brain at the speed of an overloaded neurotransmitter; her heart pounded and twitched. She was not discouraged by the ambiguity of the professor's answer, because nothing was confirmative yet. The anomaly. I was not an anomaly in Iridescia, because everybody was different there. So, I became *we*. I was willing to become *the other we*. Something has gone missing. Even if it was a nonexisting country . . . I still want to know where its non-existence came from.

The professor's coldly amiable voice cleaved her thoughts like an airplane penetrating the clouds. She was holding an opaque mask in her right hand with a thin, smoothly gleaming tube. It was attached to the white box. 'It is our duty, Fragment Number 29. Thank you so much for . . .

coming back to us,' she said, skilfully joining the two pieces of apparatus together. 'Now, Fragment Number 29, take a deep breath and relax.'

Relax? How? My muscles are always relaxed. Fragment Number 29 thought, trying to close her eyes but failed. I have no control over myself.

'And it's exactly the point,' interrupted the professor, 'you are not allowed to have any control over your body at this stage.' She pressed down the mask onto Fragment Number 29's face, covering her nose and mouth with accuracy and resourcefulness. A translucent fume released from the white box when she elevated the lever, slowly and daintily drifting towards the other end of the tube like a decolourised nimbostratus cloud.

Fragment Number 29 gasped for breath, but only inhaled more of the gas; an acrid, lancinating sensation immediately infiltrated her lungs. She screamed and wailed in silence, as if she could feel the inner membrane of her trachea stiffen and flake away before the gas swiftly reached the most vulnerable spot of her alveoli and disseminated itself into the capillaries. The white box, she recalled in despair, the white box is a gas cylinder. Stop breathing! Stop it, stop it! Stop breathing or inhale more gas, both of them will suffocate me in the end. Perhaps it is less painful to die due to the lack of oxygen.

'It is not a toxic gas, Fragment Number 29. It is therapeutic.' The professor gazed at her, still holding the lever. 'I can release more of the gas by a single movement of my thumb – it will not take more than five minutes to asphyxiate you permanently, but I am happy to make it even more efficient if you want.' She continued didactically, 'However, it will destroy your respiratory system before it inhibits the activity of your haemoglobin. Your lungs will, basically, liquefy as the gas disintegrates their membranes. Shall we wait until that moment? But I don't want you to die this early. We have not yet wrung out everything about Iridescia from you. It's impossible to hide anything, my compatriot. You better tell us now, before it's too late. What is your true feeling for Iridescia? Don't you love it? Don't you wish to go there again? Why are you so obsessed with the idea of the other country? You should have remembered the truth by now.'

An indistinct, hoarse cry leaked out from the mask. I don't know, I don't know. I cannot love it, can I? I cannot go there again, can I? You sent me to the other country, you sent me to Iridescia because Monochromia, Our Great Motherland, is at war with the other country. Her eyes convulsed open, as the very sound of *the other country* lingered on her pale lips; she finally remembered, on the verge of falling into an eternal state of self-inflicted coma, that this phrase did not come from her own memories. Everything in Iridescia did exist as an entity, but only under the aegis of a fictional world.

'Good. Not knowing the reason at all is much

more productive than making up a reason your-self, because the reason does not exist.' The professor nodded her satisfaction, and lowered the lever.

Fragment Twenty-Six

The white gas began to dissipate; the professor nestled Fragment Number 29 in her motherly arms, and petted the nape of her neck. 'I am sorry, my dearest compatriot. I am so sorry to make you go through all these *ailments*, but they are necessary for your mental health. Let us do something for you to mitigate your pain.'

'Stop the pain. Stop the pain!' Fragment Number 29 wheezed, her speech disrupted by the red-black foam oozing out from her mouth. 'Please, stop the pain, stop my breath . . . stop everything, just stop, stop, stop it!'

'Oh, we have already stopped it, Fragment Number 29.' The professor smiled, carefully wiping off the red-black foam with a white cloth. 'You can do whatever you like now, restrained by nobody. You are free.'

'No, I don't want to do anything, I can't breathe! Please, stop it, stop it . . .' Fragment Number 29 screamed faintly, her arms twitching incessantly in a convulsion of amorphous agony. 'The

215

pain does not come from my chest . . .' She lifted her arm stiffly, pointing at her head. 'It's . . . inside my brain . . . I remember, my dear professor . . . I remember, Iridescia is . . .'

'I'm always here to listen to you,' the professor said gently. 'The real pain comes from your memories of Iridescia. Now you know what I said is true. Happiness is nation-specific.'

'But the happiness I experienced in Iridescia does not disappear. Nor does the sadness. I'm tired, my professor. I have always pursued the truth, and now it's here. I don't want to face it any more.' Fragment Number 29 sobbed in silence, the professor's voice becoming more and more distant. The residual fumes in the tube slowly anesthetised her anxiety, and blurred her vision. She did not choose to remember anything, although she had almost reached the threshold of reliving the last event she witnessed before the integrity of reality fell apart. It was beyond her control. Her consciousness ascended towards the black sky, through the transparent ceiling and eventually fled away from the Intensive Care Unit.

November 2042. The progression of time had temporarily ceased, when the ending of an unfinished novel created another country in Fragment Number 29's mind.

The stainless steel gate of the Re-education Committee creaked and rattled open. A young girl wearing a white skirt entered the lecture theatre, followed by a man in black uniform. There was no expression on her face. Everybody in the lecture theatre seemed to be a duplicate of one another. Their white overalls and black scarves intricately interweaved together, generating a monochromic sea of unanimous obedience. Nobody had paid any attention to the girl; the man's stealthy footsteps were submerged in the rhythmical pounding of their booted feet.

Two men carrying a metal stretcher shuffled through the crowd. Something shrouded in black foil was lying on the stretcher, yet the girl was unable to figure out the contents inside. She stared at the men until they disappeared. Everything here looked familiar. She wondered if she had ever been here before.

The shadow-like man behind her sneered. 'Wake up, Number 29. We did not bring you here for nothing. Look at the stage. Somebody is waiting for you there.'

Everybody is shouting out something. What has enraged them? Why are they brandishing their fists? Number 29 raised her head reluctantly. I don't want to hear. What is on the stage? A woman. She was wearing a white nightgown, with some illegible words scribbled all over her emaciated body. Black cables from a dimly flickering switch panel were connected to her wrists and ankles. Number 29 noticed something viscid dribbling down from the woman's forearms; suddenly

217

she had a desire to approach the stage. As she walked closer to the crowd, the scene on the stage became less and less ambiguous. She could detect the heavy noise of her breath, as if there was a silent barrier between her and everybody else. There was another woman at the other end of the stage. She was in a white overcoat, with a black clip attached to the collar of her blouse. She is different, Number 29 thought. She is not restrained by anything, she is *free*. She should liberate the other woman, if she is free. Why is she not doing anything?

The man in black uniform clasped her arm. 'You cannot go there, Number 29,' he scowled at her, 'the lecture is in progress. All you need to do is stay here and watch what's going on. It is an important event for every one of us.'

'I am not one of those people,' Number 29 replied without looking back. 'I must see that woman. I have seen her before . . . I have seen her *here* before.'

'What the?' The man swore in undertone, flashing out a pair of manacles from his pocket. 'We will shoot you in the head if you ever dare say something like that again. Do you know who she is? If you don't behave yourself, you will spend the rest of your criminal life with her.' He wrenched Number 29's wrists with a simple, mechanical click. 'Although we are not sure if you can live that long.'

Number 29 groaned in pain; the silent barrier

collapsed and shattered when an emotionlessly sweet voice echoed in the room. The crowd was no longer howling in fury. She saw the woman blink at the audience with a loving smile, but her line of vision was concentrated on somewhere else. 'You are a bit late. We have already started the second half of the lecture.' The black clip amplified her voice, forcing the air to vibrate. 'Never mind. Thank you for bringing her here.'

'It is our duty, professor.' The man saluted, his left hand still clutching Number 29's arm. 'The first half must have been very successful. We saw the stretcher-bearers when we came in.' His voice was not loud, yet competent of travelling across the entire lecture theatre.

The woman nodded her approval, and faced the audience. 'My compatriots. The first half is merely a demonstration of our newly invented procedures for the official deletion of those renegade numbers. Every single one of us is an eyewitness to this glorious process.' She elevated her sweet voice. 'Now, it is your opportunity to implement your love for Monochromia, Our Great Motherland. However, for safety and security reasons, I am afraid that only very few of you can participate in the process.'

The majority of the audience sighed in disappointment, yet their eyes were still blazing with eagerness and agitation. Number 29 was stunned by the woman's choice of pronouns. You. I heard her use the word you, instead of we or us. Maybe she has the privilege to do so, because her voice is so beautiful.

Another man sitting in the first row stood up. He was equipped with a black clip clipped on his collar as well, but there was nothing special about his garment. 'Pardon me, professor. Ten or twelve of them should be enough. *I believe* that all of you have already prepared the necessary equipment. It is very simple.'

The professor shook her head slightly when the crowd moaned again. 'I know how much you care about the consequences of their participation as the lecturer, but we must satisfy their willingness for doing their duties. Look at them. Their brains are almost out of control.' She glanced at the crowd and laughed.

'So let them do whatever they want to the deleted number. It shouldn't take more than ten minutes,' the lecturer whispered with an ominous smile. 'Especially when Number 29 is here. I am amazed that she has not yet recognised the deleted number.'

'It is already the second year of The Great Calibration. Her collective nurturing facility must have done a good job, despite the fact that she might need to be transferred to a more professional care system.' The professor beamed back, twiddling the black cable. She looked at the woman in the nightgown compassionately. 'I am sorry, my compatriot. We shouldn't make you wait for us.' She patted the woman's trembling shoulder. 'I know you are itching to have your deletion done. Don't worry. We still love you, even if you were not the first number to be deleted. Guardian M, Our Great Leader, wants you to be happy.'

The woman smiled at the professor, and gave the audience an unfaltering stare. 'Indeed, I cannot wait for my deletion. You killed my husband, and took away my only daughter . . . but she will remember! This colour of my blood . . . is the proof of another country, the other country.' The woman took a deep breath, struggling to lift up her hands. 'My little Flora . . . my Felicity . . . please remember Iridescia, the country of colourful freedom. Wherever you are, please remember the Flower Princess and her Prince!' Her ashen face was coated with a semi-transparent membrane of dried tears and sweat, like a pallid layer of solidified limewater. Fear and hatred were throbbing in her black eyes, yet an intimidating gleam of courage had overpowered any other emotions.

The audience gasped. 'It's disgusting!' somebody in the crowd yelled, 'professor, we must delete this seditious polychromist! It's disgusting!'

The professor's face went dark. 'My compatriots! What is this colour?' She grabbed the woman's wrist; a juicy drop of something sprinkled onto her white glove. 'My research tolerates no failure,' she muttered to herself secretly, 'this degenerate number is in my control!'

'It is black!' the audience exclaimed in unison, 'everything we have is everything we have here!

Only black and white can survive, and only black and white should exist in Monochromia, Our Great Motherland! Nothing else exists, nothing else will ever exist!' Before the professor signalled her permission, a man dashed to the stage with a piercing noise of metal emitted from the grip of his hand. It was a black dagger.

Scream, scream, scream. Everybody is screaming. They have left their seats, they are desperate to play a role on the stage. Everybody has a black dagger in his grasp, including those from the last row. Down with the insurgent, down with the rebellious, down with polychromism. It is not white. Her nightgown is not white any more. The blade danced and scampered upon her chest like raging flames; red, red spikes trailed down her legs. The professor carefully placed her forefinger on a triangular button on the switch panel.

It is red. It is the colour of my blood. Number 29 shuddered at the thought of the forbidden colour. But the blood of this woman . . . She glanced at the mucilaginous liquid on the stage. A pungent odour evaporated and ascended in a graceful curve. The blood of this woman . . . is mixed with a black liquid dissolved in something else. Who is this woman? A burning sensation clung to Number 29's spine. The first *couple* of numbers to be officially deleted.

'Oh, haemoglobin, haemoglobins,' the lecturer laughed excitedly, 'but I cannot understand why Number 29 did not recognise her mother there.

And also . . . professor, are you sure that transferring Number 29 to the Centre is beneficial for the progress of The Great Calibration?'

'I do nothing without a purpose.' The professor lowered her voice. 'The purpose of transferring Number 29 is to prevent and *eliminate* further, or possible, development of polychromism in her mind, and the purpose of this black solvent is to induce pain and confusion at a higher level to the deleted number. Physical pain is much more effective than any form of verbal indoctrination – you should know this better than I do, as the lecturer. I am merely a clinical psychiatrist.'

The red and black liquids had eventually engulfed the woman's breath. A faint wail diffused into the air when she closed her eyes.

'Why . . . is my blood black?'

The crowd cheered in frenzy as the professor pressed the button.

Applause. Silence.

The professor whispered to Fragment Number 29, unconcerned about her state of consciousness. 'Faraway memories are always so captivating . . . and on the next day, you were formally delivered to our Centre.' The professor continued in a gloomy tone, with her arms crossed, 'unfortunately, that lecture turned out to be an anomaly. It was too quick; your mother died polychromic, remembering everything from her last novel, *The Other Country*. That's why our research continued until now.'

Fragment Twenty-Seven

Fragment Number 29's hand shivered. Tears flowed down her cheeks, silently and spontaneously. 'The Flower Princess and her Prince. Flora, Edwin, and Felicity Iris . . .' she murmured, 'They are . . . from my mother's novel . . .'

'You have kept your promise very well. You still remember everything from her, except your own name, Felicity, and . . .' the professor glimpsed at the doorway, and continued in an even lower voice, 'your mother's name. You have forgotten your parents' names . . . *I* have not.'

'You professor?' Fragment Number 29 said feebly, 'you know my mother?'

'Of course I do. I deleted her. She was talking about Iridescia, even before her execution. The audience was too dedicated to be distracted by her speech, but I'm not one of those people. I listened to her. I have always listened to her,' the professor replied, gazing at the black sky with a sense of pride. 'Although you didn't recognise her there, I immediately realised the importance of the term "Iridescia" for you. You're her only happiness, her *Felicity*,' she explained. 'So I decided to use that idea, when nobody seemed to have paid any attention to it. To some extent, the failure of her refilling process had resulted in the success of refilling the audience. In fact, there was no black liquid at all. What you all saw was nothing but an intricately devised optical illusion. I was not affected by it, so I remembered everything *as well*.'

The professor smiled, yet it was a different kind of smile. The semi-transparent veil of Fragment Number 29's tears had rendered it even more beautiful, under the vague shades of white illumination in the room. She detected something else hidden there. She held the professor's hand, struggling to reciprocate her with another smile. 'Thank you, Fragment Number 29. You are always . . .' laughed the professor, 'you are always tempting me to leak *my* little secrets, as if you are my . . . probably that's why you could see the images in Room Ai by yourself.'

'Images? Professor, I . . .'

'Images of a woman in purple suit at the book fair, with a blue rosette on her collar,' the professor said in a seemingly more relaxed tone. 'As you know already, it was me. A PhD student at the Capital University, canvassing for the oppositional party. We don't want that, do we? All we need is static stability, not dynamic equilibrium. What you didn't recall in Room Ai is the author's name. It's going to sound so familiar when I tell you.'

The trigger of her memories was no longer important. As long as the memory was there, its availability would vary under different circumstances. The professor's sweet voice superseded all the futile hopes for an alternative answer; it was already too late for Fragment Number 29 to stop her. She clutched the professor's palm, as if she was to go through another agonising episode of remembrance. Nothing is done without a purpose, she thought helplessly. She should have recognised the woman a long time ago.

'The author at the book fair, her name is Irene. I used to love her books. She was one of my favourite novelists, when I was about your age.'

The professor gave Fragment Number 29 a loving glance, and looked away. She had once treasured everything in the Centre, but now she could no longer experience the sense of belonging here. Time had estranged this place from her, the most important place in her life. The silvery glitter of her spectacles dimmed, when her line of vision went astray in the room. She wished she could tell Fragment Number 29 everything, assuming that they shared the same memories. 'Only if you remember, my compatriot,' she said slowly, without looking back, 'only if you have inherited all of Irene's memories.'

Fragment Number 29 did not respond instantaneously. She knew that the professor was not expecting a response anyway, either verbally or visually. The image of a woman in purple reappeared, with a different background. She was awaiting the soundless narration from the professor.

'This Centre was renamed in 2040. Its predecessor was the State Research Centre for Forensic Psychiatry. I was the youngest member.' The professor's voice synchronised with the woman, its sweet trait enhancing the youthfulness of her illusory image. Hardcover books filled up the bookshelves behind her, together with an array of framed certificates and colour photographs. A white-covered paperback was placed on a pile of folders and envelopes, somehow incompatible with the severe atmosphere of the room. She squinted at the black sky through the gap between the curtains, with a pen in her hand. A tinge of mistrust crept onto her face.

Suddenly the door rattled open, and a man in a black jacket strode in. She watched him approaching her seat calmly, without any expression of anxiety. The man glared at her, with a sly smile of victory. 'Number Nil,' he snorted, 'you need to report to the Disciplinary Committee immediately.'

The professor gave him a glacial stare. 'I'm glad that you didn't call me a Fragment,' she said. 'The Disciplinary Committee? What have I done this time?'

'Look at you,' the man shouted, ostensibly disappointed of her reaction, 'what are you wearing? And what are these photos? Are they an attempt to subvert the power of Guardian M, Our Great Leader?'

'They are from my graduation ceremony, at The Capital University.' She stood up and lowered her voice. 'Why do you ask me? Can't you remember it yourself, Fragment Number 37?'

His face went pale. He struggled to maintain his anger, as if he was practising a certain skill. 'Go to the Disciplinary Committee now!' He grabbed the book from her desk. 'Before you jeopardise the highest interests of our Centre.'

'*Your* Centre? Indeed, this place is no longer my Centre. I knew I would become the first subject of your refilling process, when the Centre lost its name.' The professor shook her head. 'It's only a book, Fragment Number 37. It's purely fictional. Where is your copy? I remember seeing you conversing with its author.'

'Shut up! It's the evidence of your crime! The Great Calibration has already began, and I'm doing my duties as a glorious citizen of Monochromia, Our Great Motherland.' fragment Number 37 yelled, and flung the book against the wall. He clasped the professor's wrists, trying to frogmarch her out of the room.

The professor did not resist. 'What will you do? If you refill me, your Centre will lose the capability of refilling anybody else.' She shuffled towards the door. 'You're obviously very proud of yourself. What can you get by reporting me?'

'Because I could not get you, when we were at university together. I cannot love you, but *we* can,' Fragment Number 37 said in a sullen tone. 'So I reported you, because I know you well enough. You must learn to protect yourself.'

'Thank you for your kind advice,' the professor smiled. 'Before I leave my office, can I look at it for the last time?'

Fragment Number 37 nodded reluctantly. 'You have never changed, Number Nil. It has been a real pleasure to work with you. We can not afford to let you go.'

The professor gazed at her bookshelves with a deep sigh. 'Is it something regretful? Perhaps I'll still be your colleague after my refilling. I will be much more dedicated to your Centre.' She turned back to the man. 'I have always loved this place, ever since I first joined it. Now I will have to betray it.'

'It's not a betrayal. You will always belong to our Centre. We still need you because we love you, Number Nil.'

The door closed as soon as they went out. The purple colour of her suit vanished into the prevailing black shadow outside the room, like a drop of clean water dissolving in the sea of darkness. Fragment Number 29 hid her face under the duvet, bringing an unwilling end to the episode.

'What happened?' asked the professor. 'What did you see?'

'This cannot be true, my professor,' Fragment Number 29 sobbed, 'he cannot have betrayed you. Did you feel hurt?'

The professor raised her eyebrow. 'Why? You're too naive, Fragment Number 29. Betrayal is everywhere. You have to be vindictive to be sincere. He had never predicted that one day I would demote him, sending him away from the Centre. He's now the visiting inspector to the Centre, but it's nothing more than a puppet.'

'He loved you,' Fragment Number 29 said, peeking at the professor. 'How could he ever have reported you, because of . . . my mother's book?'

'He did not love me. He reported me only because the Centre needed me,' answered the professor. 'They needed my expertise to refill people like you. I can hardly remember what happened to me afterwards, but now I can tell that my own refilling process wasn't very successful either. It had produced one side effect. I'm still doing my duties here, to be honest. You are the last one to be refilled, my compatriot.'

Fragment Number 29 leaned towards the professor, looking at her with sympathy. 'Does it mean the Centre will no longer need you after you've refilled me?' She held the professor's hand; she felt no warmth underneath her white gloves.

'Probably yes,' said the professor. 'All of us will fall into the state of collective amnesia, when your refilling has completed. None of us – including me – will remember anything about The Great Calibration.'

'So everybody will be happy then. It's hard for me to believe in my own beliefs now.' Fragment Number 29 half-closed her eyes. 'If Iridescia is not real I don't know what to believe.'

'The novel is not finished. We can make corrections to the book at our discretion.' The professor smiled, fondling Fragment Number 29's hair. 'You have proved that most of your beliefs are deviated from the reality; but there's one detail that you have missed out, and that is the key to the success of your refilling. Would you like to know?' She paused, waiting for a response from Fragment Number 29.

'Yes, I would, my professor,' Fragment Number 29 replied in a determined manner.

'You did not recognise your mother at her deletion, and that was due to the repression of your memories,' the professor resumed with satisfaction. 'But someone else was also missing there. What name would you associate with Irene?'

A flashback of two stretcher-bearers carrying something in black foil disrupted Fragment Number 29's speech. Nobody had revealed the contents inside it, even if she made an instinctive presumption that her father was deleted before her mother. She gasped in a spasm of fearful anticipation.

Fragment Twenty-Eight

A black cumulus cloud descended from the black sky, through the glass ceiling and eventually landed at Fragment Number 29's bedside. It reformed automatically into a man in a black uniform. His blond hair beamed with a metallic shine, his emerald eyes burned with darkness. Fragment Number 29 quivered when he spoke – not directly to her, but to the professor. He had never given a single glance at her.

'How is her refilling, professor? Have we finished yet?'

The professor held his hand; his black leather glove cast a dark shadow onto her white sleeves. 'You've disturbed our conversation,' she stroked his fringe, 'I'm pleased to see you here, Fragment Number 809. I like your *black* hair, and black eyes . . . I can see myself there.'

'Fragment Number 809? No, his name is Edwin Iris!' Fragment Number 29 cried, struggling to move her body. She stared at her strange beloved, looking startled by his kind nonchalance. Even the air surrounding him had become something different, something no longer reminiscent of his iridescent characteristics.

'His name *was* Edwin Iris, but he has chosen to become a Fragment,' the professor said proudly. 'I envy him sometimes, because he still remembers that name. I had nothing to prove my identity, except Number Nil, a derelict Fragment.'

'No, I promise, I will forget it one day,' said Edwin Iris, 'please trust me.'

Fragment Number 29 sobbed in desperation. 'How did you let it happen, Edwin? What have they done to you? When did you . . .'

'Don't call me Edwin. I have been working for the professor and the Centre, ever since your mother was deleted. Now I'm with you again, Fragment Number 29, to tell you the truth.'

'But I have not yet made our promise come true. I have not brought another colour to Monochromia . . . Our Great Motherland,' Fragment Number 29 muttered, with an irritating sensation in her throat. Fatigue overwhelmed her brain; she curled up and pulled up the duvet. I wish I could change the truth, she thought. She gazed at her hands, as if she could see her own memories being sieved through her fingers. Edwin Iris was from the other place. She was here, only to meet him again, only to become the other 'we' again. Who is this 'we'? she cried out in silence, Where is 'the other place'?

'The truth comes from nowhere, my compatriot, because it's variable.' The professor came towards her, knelt down and smiled. 'For example, your mother had created Iridescia in her novel, and it had converted itself into a delusional entity in your mind. All your thoughts and ideas are based upon a single belief that there is another country, an obsession almost leading you to the edge of an emotional breakdown. You'd have totally lost your sanity without our protection.'

'So you're refilling me with *your* truth?' Fragment Number 29 whispered, tranquilised by the warm tenderness of the professor's voice.

The professor slowly shook her head. 'You were not the only person suffering from this disorder before The Calibration. The refilling process is not targeted at the faulty ideas, you must understand. Ideas themselves might not be susceptible to reformation, but the people behind them are.'

The people behind them. Fragment number 29 looked away, when she felt that the accumulation of tears was going out of control. My mother wasn't cured during the Calibration, so she had infected me with those painful ideas. Should I hate her? She quivered, frightened by her own thought.

'Now, my compatriot. Fragment Number 809 will not interrupt us any more, can you tell me the answer to my question?' the professor said abruptly, 'what is the name associated with Irene?'

Fragment Number 29 blinked, confused by the

reminder of their conversation. Somehow she wished that Edwin *would* interrupt. He stood by the door like a black celluloid figurine, threatening yet flimsy. She thought of the man in navy blue shirt, eating fruitcakes in the garden. 'Mitchell,' she uttered the word without realising it, 'my father.'

'Correct,' the professor beamed her satisfaction. 'Where do you think he is?'

'He's dead, he's dead, isn't he? He was deleted by the Re-education Committee, he's dead!' Fragment Number 29 blubbered, 'you know this, don't you? Why do you ask me? Please, I can't stand this any more. I don't want to know!'

The professor stood up, calmly walking towards Edwin Iris. 'Don't panic. You need to know, Fragment Number 29. Did you witness his deletion? You didn't. The incorrect cognition of facts is at the root of your maladaptive behaviour. Sadly, you still seem to be unaware of the real situation. Your father was the co-creator of Iridescia, would you trust him more than us?'

Fragment Number 29 did not have the chance to respond. She saw the professor opening the door, yet unable to rescue herself from the room. The effects of the suffocating fluid in her chest had not completely disseminated, and she was too afraid to make any movement. The Intensive Care Unit was her only shelter, the only place where she could escape from the electrical shocks in Room Ai. She knew she was to be confronted with another stimulus of distress, but emotional pain was far less detrimental than bodily harm. Trust. This word seemed so heavy, so heartbreaking that she couldn't even bear its sound. She looked at Edwin Iris, trying to figure out if there was any cryptic message under his sober expression. She was almost comforted by the fact that he had sacrificed his identity, yet she was unwilling to admit such a feeling. Everybody would eventually be equal, when the other country descended into nothingness. His colours were no more superior to hers, so she should be happy. Fragments, we are all Fragments, she thought. She finally had the courage to sit up again, when a distorted smile concealed her tears.

A man in a black suit came into the room. He was wearing the same black scarf as the professor's, with a delicate nuance of style; the golden frame of his spectacles almost scintillating under the luminous ceiling. Fragment Number 29 could hardly hear their footsteps. Edwin Iris followed him, and saluted when he sat down in the white armchair next to the bed. The professor stood behind him, staring into the vacuum of Edwin's eyes.

The man inclined forward and embraced Fragment Number 29. 'You look so different,' he whispered, 'I have nearly forgotten.'

Fragment Number 29 faked a blank smile, even though something bitter was smouldering deep inside her mind. 'Who are you?' She stammered, as if the man's appearance had severed her voice.

'My name is Mitchell. I am . . . from Iridescia,' the man said with a professional subtlety. 'Welcome home, my Felicity.'

'No . . . Iridescia . . . Iridescia does not exist! You cannot, you cannot be . . . my . . .'

Fragment Number 29 grasped the man's hands, trembling in excitement and doubt. Everything, everything had come back to her when she felt the warm bloodstream underneath the man's skin, and the lively colour of his capillaries. He is Mitchell, his name is Mitchell! She placed his hands on her cheeks, and drew in a short breath. His face was wrinkled, his hair faded with age; but nothing could change the paternal gentleness demonstrated in his bright eyes. 'Father,' she started to weep, 'I'm here . . . your Felicity is here. Why haven't you come earlier? I've been waiting for so long, waiting for you to bring me back . . .'

'I have always been here, my Felicity,' smiled Mitchell. 'Why do you think that Iridescia doesn't exist?'

'Because I thought . . . I thought I would never see you again, father,' Fragment Number 29 cried, leaning against his shoulder. 'Please take me out of the Centre, I want to go back to Iridescia . . . no matter whether it exists or not.'

Mitchell caressed her back with a deep sigh. 'If you leave the Centre, you will never be able to go anywhere. Our Centre *is* Iridescia.' He wiped the tears from her face. 'We have created everything for you, because we want you to be happy. Everything is contained under the black sky, the invincible airspace of Monochromia, Our Great Motherland. However, this does not imply that Iridescia isn't real.'

'So we are in Iridescia now? Father, I'm confused, where are we exactly? Is there a different country? Is there only one country?' Fragment Number 29 snuggled up to his chest, oblivious of everything else in the room. She wanted nobody else. The mere presence of her father had liberated her from all her fears and anxieties, for the past and the future. She could hear the clock ticking again, defrozen from the darkest day in November 2042.

'We are in Iridescia,' Mitchell continued, 'the other country *within* Monochromia, Our Great Motherland. There are certain things that cannot coexist, so we have made them a part of us – not apart from us. The idea of Iridescia in your mother's novel can never exist in harmony with our Motherland. The point is that there could be more than one name for the place, but there is only one "we". Iridescia is one of us, Fragment Number 809 is one of us . . . I am one of us, my Felicity.'

'This "we" . . . is not Iridescia. I can't see the colours, or the flowers in our garden. Do you not miss them, father?' asked Fragment Number 29, with cautious expectation, 'do you not remember?'

'I do remember, my Felicity. But my memories do not affect my logic. You must understand that everything is changeable, especially people. Trust me, Iridescia has never been a country of colours. Irene and I visited there before you were born, and it was completely different from what she's told you from the book. In fact, it was the opposite.'

'Really?' Fragment Number 29 lowered her voice. 'Before I was born . . . so it must have been somewhere outside Monochromia.'

Mitchell put a finger to her lips. 'Monochromia, Our Great Motherland,' he whispered, 'has always been here. It was indeed a shame that Irene did not believe me, because she had developed the same psychiatric disorder when writing her last novel. So she was deleted for a due cause . . . but you're innocent, my Felicity. What you need is treatment, not deletion. My dedicated colleagues at the Centre have finally reached the last stage of your refilling.'

Fragment Number 29's arms twitched, as if they were repelled by an undetectable force inside Mitchell. She turned her head to the professor in a mechanical posture. A chilling impulse travelled down her spine, and collided violently with the warm comfort that had already been installed by him. She wanted to scream, yet incapable of controlling her own voice. She was absolutely certain that the man sitting next to her was her father, the last person she could ever trust; so she decided to protect such trust by modifying her own realisations, in the devout hope that she could resolve the paradox by drawing an equal sign between two antagonistic names.

Fragment Twenty-Nine

'I have always loved Irene, but I loved her even more after the beginning of The Great Calibration. When we were being re-educated at the Committee, I eventually realised how important she was to me. So I wanted to save her . . . and you, my Felicity. It was the most painful moment for me, when I ordered your refilling process.'

Mitchell stood between the professor and Edwin Iris, with arms crossed. His voice was soft as ever; every word he spoke was a consolation for Fragment Number 29. The meanings of the words had no further implications, it was the speaker that really mattered for her. Tears formed a diaphanous veil before her eyes. She stared at them, assuming that the distance between them would never extend again. The professor held Mitchell at his waist, and she saw Edwin Iris smile. Another perfect image, she thought. She was tired of being an observer; she was desperate to join them, to become a part of the perfect composition. They all looked so happy. Yes, they must be. They were from Iridescia.

'Irene had betrayed me,' said Mitchell, satisfied with the professor's intimacy. 'All I have is you, my Felicity. I did everything I could to help you, to treat your illness. I know it had been an unpleasant process, but the product justifies the procedure. You have not disappointed us.'

Fragment Number 29 bent over, sobbingly kissed her father's black scarf. 'I thought I was hopeless,' she cried, 'I'm so sorry . . . I must confess that I have betrayed you, too. I don't deserve your love, because . . . I thought Iridescia had colours, I thought it was a country of freedom.'

'It is a country of freedom, because it belongs to Monochromia, Our Great Motherland,' smiled Mitchell. 'You have everything here. The Centre, Iridescia and Our Great Motherland. This sequence will never be altered. Irene tried to reverse the order, but she failed. Iridescia was an idealised world for her, and it's not the fact. Sometimes it's totally unnecessary to distinguish the fictional and the real, but it is vital for us to understand that only the reality is dominant.'

'That's because . . . mother was ill, like me. I'm so happy that I've begun to detach myself from my delusions, and be refilled with the reality.' Fragment Number 29 looked up to the professor. 'Thank you.'

The professor glanced at Mitchell. 'You're always a part of us, Fragment Number 29. We will always be with you at the Centre, because the concept of *we* is eternal.'

'You're here, safe and secure,' Mitchell resumed. 'I was determined to give you a better future, when I deserted writing and studied psychiatry instead. The Centre offered me the opportunity to help more people like you during the Calibration, and I succeeded. See, all of us are committed to your happiness. Now you don't have to worry about separating from any of us. We are all here.' He held the professor's gloved hands, and hugged her. 'Like a big family.'

Fragment Number 29 stretched out her arm to the professor, somehow jealous of her being so close to her father. She was happy to see them together, even though she still felt a little lonely. Edwin Iris stepped forward and sat next to her.

'Edwin?' Fragment Number 29 lowered her head, surprised by his sudden movement. 'Sorry . . . I mean, Fragment Number 809.'

Edwin placed his hand on her frail shoulder. His warmth penetrated through his black leather glove, soothingly flowing into her body. 'My Flora,' he whispered, their fingers interlocking together, 'I will never leave you again. Everything we have is everything we have here. I will be with you forever, because now I am Monochromian. Black and white are more beautiful than any other colours, so we don't need Iridescia anymore, do we?'

'No, we don't, of course we don't. All I need is you, Edwin. Wherever we are. I love you, Edwin,' Fragment Number 29 whimpered, and embraced him with all her strength. She kissed him, again and again. The cold reflection of her white night-gown on his black uniform melted into a harmonious swirl of peaceful reconciliation; she did not notice the red spikes at the centre. They were all something of the past, and the past had already vanished, like the common name of *Amaranthus caudatus.*

'My Felicity,' said Mitchell, gently patting her back, 'the professor and I have been working together for nearly ten years. She had given up many chances of promotion, because she cared about you more than your mother did.'

'Irene was rather irresponsible, wasn't she?' the professor replied, 'to pressurise her own daughter, only because of her individualistic fallacies.'

'She never changed,' Mitchell shrugged, 'no matter how much I loved her, she was too obsessed to be considerate. Sometimes I wish I'd met you earlier, my dear professor.'

The professor blushed; Fragment Number 29 gazed at her, intrigued by that strange colour on her face. It must be another shade of grey. 'We all love one another,' she said, 'I can't let any of us to be unhappy.'

I am happy. Fragment Number 29 thought, I have never been so happy before. She couldn't understand why it took her so long to realise such a basic fact, that polychromism was the only trigger of all unhappiness; she felt guilty for her ignorance. Here. Nowhere. Everywhere . . . Iridescia was created by our Centre, and our Centre belonged to Monochromia, Our Great Motherland.

'Ring around the roses, a pocketful of posies. A-tishoo, A-tishoo, we all fall down,' she murmured, pleased with the second half of the rhyme. She stared at her wrist, observing the shadowy colour of her capillaries. It was not the colour of amaranthus, but she was frightened by the tiniest trace of uncertainty inside her blood vessels. She wanted to do something for the Centre, in order to demonstrate her gratitude.

'I think the crisis has been successfully resolved,' said Mitchell, glancing at the professor. 'It seems that you have remembered more about the *real* Iridescia than everybody else.'

'Because I was such a faithful reader of both you and Irene's books,' the professor laughed satirically. 'But there is no point in remembering the unwanted memories. Monochromia, Our Great Motherland, is no longer at war with Iridescia.'

'You have done very well, Number Nil. As the first subject to be calibrated in the Centre, you have proved your loyalty and dedication.' Mitchell grinned, giving the professor an insinuating look.

The professor took off her gloves, revealing the black scars underneath. 'Now you can trust me, sir. I hope the Centre will continue to utilise its expertise, even after the case of both Fragment Number 29 and I. My calibration had resulted in the dissociation of my identity, and had produced another *I*.'

'The other *you* is the refilled form of Fragment Number 29, the immaculate self. It certainly has been a time-consuming process. Fortunately, we can now proceed to the final stage.' Mitchell smiled, and slowly took out a scalpel from the pocket inside his suit. He removed the cap carefully.

The professor looked at Fragment Number 29 empathetically. 'Are you my mirror image?' she murmured, without expecting an answer from her. She did not need to know.

Fragment Number 29 turned back. 'Father, Edwin said he will plant some black and white flowers for me,' she said excitedly, 'do you mind, father?'

'No, of course I don't. I know you like flowers, especially the black ones. They are in the colour of our blood.' Mitchell kissed her forehead; his hands crept up her back, and gently capsulated her neck. He appreciated her defenceless position. 'We love you, Fragment Number 29. You are our Felicity, our Flora.'

The scalpel entered Fragment Number 29's jugular vein; she did not feel painful, as if it was something purely natural for her. She saw the crimson spikes trickling from her shoulder like a garland of amaryllis, sprinkling her bed with tiny droplets of liquefied garnet. She narrowed her eyes in a seizure of euphoria. 'Now I can finally prove that my blood is black, too. Just like you. Just like everybody else.' she whispered proudly to the professor. 'I am having a friendly conversation with my own voice. I have become *we*. How much more can I love you, Monochromia, Our Great Motherland? You have cured my illness. I will never dream again, I promise.'

Her field of vision froze, like a snapshot of her own family; she was under the guardianship of her father's arms, with the professor and Edwin Iris watching her. Everybody she loved was here. Nothing else existed, and nothing else would ever exist. Her voice faded into the monochromic air, and congealed itself as the everlasting indication of her happiness. Iridescia was monochromic, and so is our blood. She felt the sweet touch of Edwin's lips, and the fragrant smile from the professor. Everything seemed to be a reward for her. She had won the battle for us.